DRACULA'S GUEST

AND
OTHER DEADLY TALES

DRACULA'S GUEST

AND
OTHER DEADLY TALES

BRAM STOKER

Illustrated by
ERIC SHANOWER

HUNGRY TIGER PRESS
PORTLAND, OR

Dracula's Guest and Other Deadly Tales
is published by

HUNGRY TIGER PRESS
314 SE 129th Avenue, Portland, OR 97233

ISBN 978-1-929527-33-5

These stories are over a hundred years old and reflect societal attitudes of their time. Several stories, in particular "The Squaw," contain attitudes, terms, and portrayals of race, gender, and ethnicity that are offensive.

www.HungryTigerPress.store

CONTENTS

DRACULA'S GUEST

WHEN WE STARTED for our drive, the sun was shining brightly on Munich, and the air was full of the joyousness of early summer. Just as we were about to depart, Herr Delbrück (the *maître d'hôtel* of the Quatre Saisons, where I was staying) came down, bareheaded, to the carriage and, after wishing me a pleasant drive, said to the coachman, still holding his hand on the handle of the carriage door:

"Remember you are back by nightfall. The sky looks bright but there is a shiver in the north wind that says there may be a sudden storm. But I am sure you will not be late." Here he smiled, and added, "for you know what night it is."

Johann answered with an emphatic, "Ja, mein Herr," and, touching his hat, drove off quickly. When we had cleared the town, I said, after signaling to him to stop:

"Tell me, Johann, what is tonight?"

He crossed himself, as he answered laconically: "Walpurgis Nacht." Then he took out his watch, a great, old-fashioned German silver thing as big as a turnip, and looked at it, with his eyebrows gathered together and a little impatient shrug of his shoulders. I realized that this was his way of respectfully protesting against the unnecessary delay, and sank back in the carriage, merely motioning him to proceed. He started off rapidly, as if to make up for lost time. Every now and then the horses seemed to throw up their heads and sniffed the air suspiciously. On such occasions I often looked round in alarm. The road was pretty bleak, for we were traversing a sort of high, wind-swept plateau. As we drove, I saw a road that looked but little used, and which seemed to dip through a little, winding valley. It looked so inviting that, even at the risk of offending him, I called Johann to stop — and when he had pulled up, I told him I would like to drive down that road. He made all sorts of excuses, and frequently crossed himself as he spoke. This somewhat piqued my curiosity, so I asked him various questions. He answered fencingly, and repeatedly looked at his watch in protest. Finally, I said:

"Well, Johann, I want to go down this road. I shall not ask you to come unless you like; but tell me why you do not like to go, that is all I ask." For answer he seemed to throw himself off the box, so quickly did he reach the ground. Then he stretched out his hands appealingly to me, and implored me not to go. There was just enough of English mixed with the German for me to understand the drift of his talk. He seemed always just about to tell me something — the very idea of which evidently frightened him; but each time he pulled himself up, saying, as he crossed himself: "Walpurgis Nacht!"

I tried to argue with him, but it was difficult to argue with a man when I did not know his language. The advantage certainly rested with him, for although he began to speak in English, of a very crude and broken kind, he always got excited and broke into his native tongue—and every time he did so, he looked at his watch. Then the horses became restless and sniffed the air. At this he grew very pale, and, looking around in a frightened way, he suddenly jumped forward, took them by the bridles and led them on some twenty feet. I followed, and asked why he had done this. For answer he crossed himself, pointed to the spot we had left and drew his carriage in the direction of the other road, indicating a cross, and said, first in German, then in English: "Buried him—him what killed themselves."

I remembered the old custom of burying suicides at cross-roads: "Ah! I see, a suicide. How interesting!" But for the life of me I could not make out why the horses were frightened.

Whilst we were talking, we heard a sort of sound between a yelp and a bark. It was far away; but the horses got very restless, and it took Johann all his time to quiet them. He was pale, and said, "It sounds like a wolf—but yet there are no wolves here now."

"No?" I said, questioning him; "isn't it long since the wolves were so near the city?"

"Long, long," he answered, "in the spring and summer; but with the snow the wolves have been here not so long."

Whilst he was petting the horses and trying to quiet them, dark clouds drifted rapidly across the sky. The sunshine passed away, and a breath of cold wind seemed to drift past us. It was only a breath, however, and more in the nature of a warning than a fact, for the sun came out brightly again. Johann looked under his lifted hand at the horizon and said:

"The storm of snow, he comes before long time." Then he looked at his watch again, and, straightway holding his reins firmly — for the horses were still pawing the ground restlessly and shaking their heads — he climbed to his box as though the time had come for proceeding on our journey.

I felt a little obstinate and did not at once get into the carriage.

"Tell me," I said, "about this place where the road leads," and I pointed down.

Again he crossed himself and mumbled a prayer, before he answered, "It is unholy."

"What is unholy?" I enquired.

"The village."

"Then there is a village?"

"No, no. No one lives there hundreds of years."

My curiosity was piqued, "But you said there was a village."

"There was."

"Where is it now?"

Whereupon he burst out into a long story in German and English, so mixed up that I could not quite understand exactly what he said, but roughly I gathered that long ago, hundreds of years, men had died there and been buried in their graves; and sounds were heard under the clay, and when the graves were opened, men and women were found rosy with life, and their mouths red with blood. And so, in haste to save their lives (aye, and their souls! — and here he crossed himself) those who were left fled away to other places, where the living lived, and the dead were dead and not — not something. He was evidently afraid to speak the last words. As he proceeded with his narration, he grew more and more excited. It seemed as if his imagination had got hold of him, and he ended in

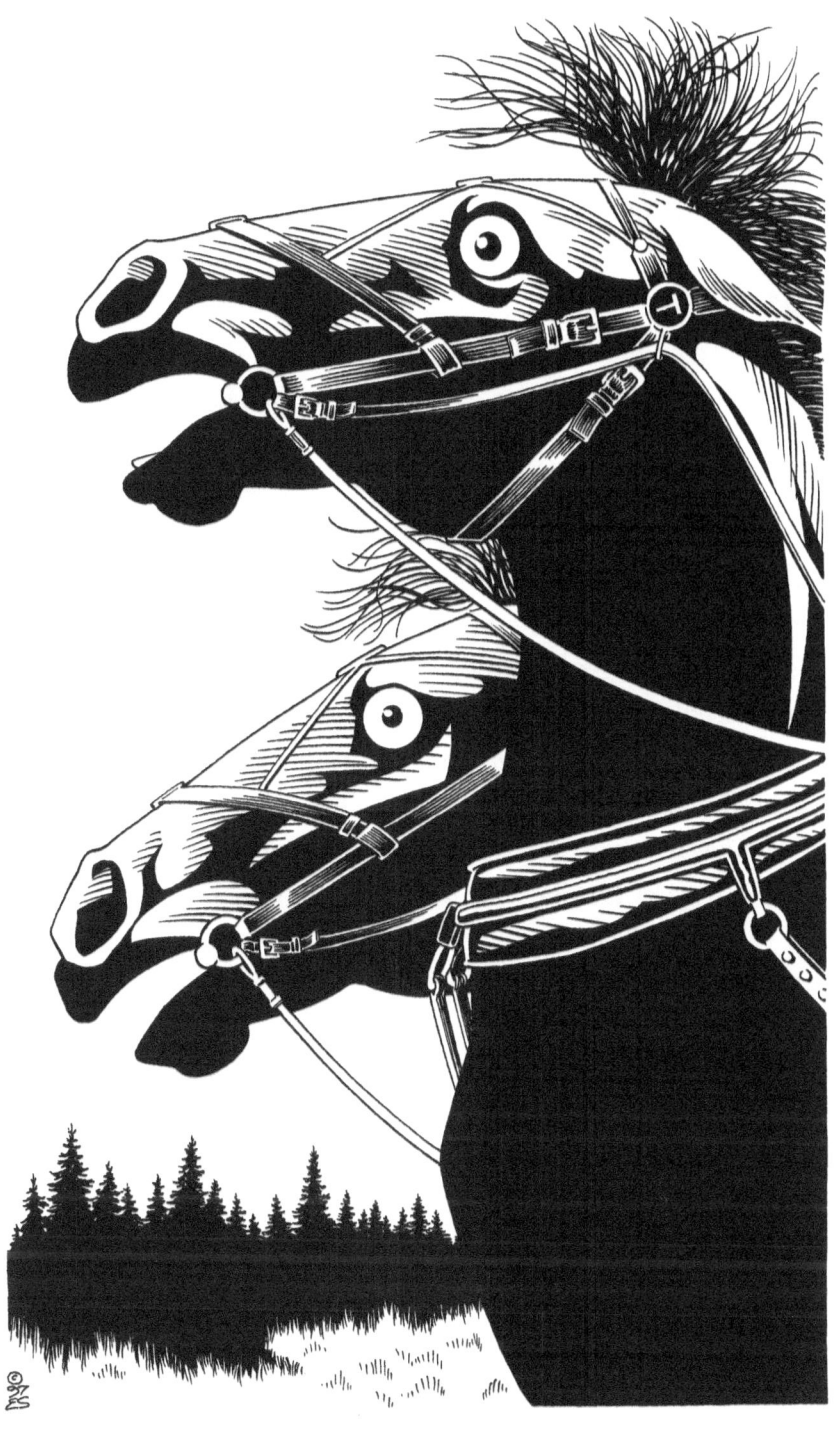

a perfect paroxysm of fear — white-faced, perspiring, trembling and looking round him, as if expecting that some dreadful presence would manifest itself there in the bright sunshine on the open plain. Finally, in an agony of desperation, he cried:

"Walpurgis Nacht!" and pointed to the carriage for me to get in.

All my English blood rose at this, and, standing back, I said:

"You are afraid, Johann — you are afraid. Go home; I shall return alone; the walk will do me good." The carriage door was open. I took from the seat my oak walking-stick — which I always carry on my holiday excursions — and closed the door, pointing back to Munich, and said, "Go home, Johann — Walpurgis Nacht doesn't concern Englishmen."

The horses were now more restive than ever, and Johann was trying to hold them in, while excitedly imploring me not to do anything so foolish. I pitied the poor fellow, he was deeply in earnest; but all the same I could not help laughing. His English was quite gone now. In his anxiety he had forgotten that his only means of making me understand was to talk my language, so he jabbered away in his native German. It began to be a little tedious. After giving the direction, "Home!" I turned to go down the cross-road into the valley.

With a despairing gesture, Johann turned his horses towards Munich. I leaned on my stick and looked after him. He went slowly along the road for a while: then there came over the crest of the hill a man tall and thin. I could see so much in the distance. When he drew near the horses, they began to jump and kick about, then to scream with terror. Johann could not hold them in; they bolted down the road, running away madly. I watched them out of sight, then looked for the stranger, but I found that he, too, was gone.

With a light heart I turned down the side road through the deepening valley to which Johann had objected. There was not the slightest reason, that I could see, for his objection; and I daresay I tramped for a couple of hours without thinking of time or distance, and certainly without seeing a person or a house. So far as the place was concerned, it was desolation itself. But I did not notice this particularly till, on turning a bend in the road, I came upon a scattered fringe of wood; then I recognized that I had been impressed unconsciously by the desolation of the region through which I had passed.

I sat down to rest myself, and began to look around. It struck me that it was considerably colder than it had been at the commencement of my walk—a sort of sighing sound seemed to be around me, with, now and then, high overhead, a sort of muffled roar. Looking upwards I noticed that great thick clouds were drifting rapidly across the sky from North to South at a great height. There were signs of coming storm in some lofty stratum of the air. I was a little chilly, and, thinking that it was the sitting still after the exercise of walking, I resumed my journey.

The ground I passed over was now much more picturesque. There were no striking objects that the eye might single out; but in all there was a charm of beauty. I took little heed of time and it was only when the deepening twilight forced itself upon me that I began to think of how I should find my way home. The brightness of the day had gone. The air was cold, and the drifting of clouds high overhead was more marked. They were accompanied by a sort of far-away rushing sound, through which seemed to come at intervals that mysterious cry which the driver had said came from a wolf. For a while I hesitated. I had said I would see the deserted village, so on I went, and presently came on a wide stretch of open country, shut in by hills all around. Their sides were covered with trees which spread down to the plain, dotting, in clumps, the gentler slopes and hollows which showed here and there. I followed with my eye the winding of the road, and saw that it curved close to one of the densest of these clumps and was lost behind it.

As I looked there came a cold shiver in the air, and the snow began to fall. I thought of the miles and miles of bleak country I had passed, and then hurried on to seek the shelter of the wood in front. Darker and darker grew the sky, and faster and heavier fell the snow, till the earth before and around me was a glistening white carpet the further edge of which was lost in misty vagueness. The road was here but crude, and when on the level its boundaries were not so marked, as when it passed through the cuttings; and in a little while I found that I must have strayed from it, for I missed underfoot the hard surface, and my feet sank deeper in the grass and moss. Then the wind grew stronger and blew with ever increasing force, till I was fain to run before it. The air became icy-cold, and in spite of my exercise I began to suffer. The snow was now falling so thickly and whirling around me in such rapid eddies that I could hardly keep my eyes open. Every now and then the heavens were torn asunder by vivid lightning, and in the flashes, I could see ahead of me a great mass of trees, chiefly yew and cypress all heavily coated with snow.

I was soon amongst the shelter of the trees, and there, in comparative silence, I could hear the rush of the wind high overhead. Presently the blackness of the storm had become merged in the darkness of the night. By-and-by the storm seemed to be passing away: it now only came in fierce puffs or blasts. At such moments

the weird sound of the wolf appeared to be echoed by many similar sounds around me.

Now and again, through the black mass of drifting cloud, came a straggling ray of moonlight, which lit up the expanse, and showed me that I was at the edge of a dense mass of cypress and yew trees. As the snow had ceased to fall, I walked out from the shelter and began to investigate more closely. It appeared to me that, amongst so many old foundations as I had passed, there might be still standing a house in which, though in ruins, I could find some sort of shelter for a while. As I skirted the edge of the copse, I found that a low wall encircled it, and following this I presently found an opening. Here the cypresses formed an alley leading up to a square mass of some kind of building. Just as I caught sight of this, however, the drifting clouds obscured the moon, and I passed up the path in darkness. The wind must have grown colder, for I felt myself shiver as I walked; but there was hope of shelter, and I groped my way blindly on.

I stopped, for there was a sudden stillness. The storm had passed; and, perhaps in sympathy with nature's silence, my heart seemed to cease to beat. But this was only momentarily; for suddenly the moonlight broke through the clouds, showing me that I was in a graveyard, and that the square object before me was a great massive tomb of marble, as white as the snow that lay on and all around it. With the moonlight there came a fierce sigh of the storm, which appeared to resume its course with a long, low howl, as of many dogs or wolves. I was awed and shocked, and felt the cold perceptibly grow upon me till it seemed to grip me by the heart. Then while the flood of moonlight still fell on the marble tomb, the storm gave further evidence of renewing, as though it was returning on its track. Impelled by some sort of fascination, I approached the sepulchre to see what it was, and why such a thing stood alone in such a place. I walked around it, and read, over the Doric door, in German:

> COUNTESS DOLINGEN OF GRATZ
> IN STYRIA
> SOUGHT AND FOUND DEATH
> 1801

On the top of the tomb, seemingly driven through the solid marble — for the structure was composed of a few vast blocks of stone — was a great iron spike or stake. On going to the back I saw, graven in great Russian letters:

> "The dead travel fast."

There was something so weird and uncanny about the whole thing that it gave me a turn and made me feel quite faint. I began to wish, for the first time, that I had taken Johann's advice. Here a thought struck me, which came under almost mysterious circumstances and with a terrible shock. This was Walpurgis Night!

Walpurgis Night, when, according to the belief of millions of people, the Devil was abroad — when the graves were opened and the dead came forth and walked. When all evil things of earth and air and water held revel. This very place the driver had specially shunned. This was the depopulated village of centuries ago. This was where the suicide lay; and this was the place where I was alone — unmanned, shivering with cold in a shroud of snow with a wild storm gathering again upon me! It took all my philosophy, all the religion I had been taught, all my courage, not to collapse in a paroxysm of fright.

And now a perfect tornado burst upon me. The ground shook as though thousands of horses thundered across it; and this time the storm bore on its icy wings, not snow, but great hailstones which drove with such violence that they might have come from the thongs of Balearic slingers — hailstones that beat down leaf and branch and made the shelter of the cypresses of no more avail than though their stems were standing-corn. At the first I had rushed to the nearest tree; but I was soon fain to leave it and seek the only spot that seemed to afford refuge, the deep Doric doorway of the marble tomb. There, crouching against the massive bronze door, I gained a certain amount of protection from the beating of the hailstones, for now they only drove against me as they ricocheted from the ground and the side of the marble.

As I leaned against the door, it moved slightly and opened inwards. The shelter of even a tomb was welcome in that pitiless tempest, and I was about to enter it when there came a flash of forked-lightning that lit up the whole expanse of the heavens. In the instant, as I am a living man, I saw, as my eyes were turned into the darkness of the tomb, a beautiful woman, with rounded cheeks and red lips, seemingly sleeping on a bier. As the thunder broke overhead, I was grasped as by the hand of a giant and hurled out into the storm. The whole thing was so sudden that, before I could realize the shock, moral as well as physical, I found the hailstones beating me down. At the same time, I had a strange, dominating feeling that I was not alone. I looked towards the tomb. Just then there came another blinding flash, which seemed to strike the iron

stake that surmounted the tomb and to pour through to the earth, blasting and crumbling the marble, as in a burst of flame. The dead woman rose for a moment of agony, while she was lapped in the flame, and her bitter scream of pain was drowned in the thunder-crash. The last thing I heard was this mingling of dreadful sound, as again I was seized in the giant-grasp and dragged away, while the hailstones beat on me, and the air around seemed reverberant with the howling of wolves. The last sight that I remembered was a vague, white, moving mass, as if all the graves around me had sent out the phantoms of their sheeted-dead, and that they were closing in on me through the white cloudiness of the driving hail.

Gradually there came a sort of vague beginning of conscious-ness; then a sense of weariness that was dreadful. For a time, I re-membered nothing; but slowly my senses returned. My feet seemed positively racked with pain, yet I could not move them. They seemed to be numbed. There was an icy feeling at the back of my neck and all down my spine, and my ears, like my feet, were dead, yet in torment; but there was in my breast a sense of warmth which was, by comparison, delicious. It was as a nightmare—a physical nightmare, if one may use such an expression; for some heavy weight on my chest made it difficult for me to breathe.

This period of semi-lethargy seemed to remain a long time, and as it faded away, I must have slept or swooned. Then came a sort of loathing, like the first stage of sea-sickness, and a wild desire to be free from something—I knew not what. A vast stillness enveloped me, as though all the world were asleep or dead—only broken by the low panting as of some animal close to me. I felt a warm rasping at my throat, then came a consciousness of the awful truth, which chilled me to the heart and sent the blood surging up through my brain. Some great animal was lying on me and now licking my throat. I feared to stir, for some instinct of prudence bade me lie still; but the brute seemed to realize that there was now some change in me, for it raised its head. Through my eyelashes I saw above me the two great flaming eyes of a gigantic wolf. Its sharp white teeth gleamed in the gaping red mouth, and I could feel its hot breath fierce and acrid upon me.

For another spell of time, I remembered no more. Then I became conscious of a low growl, followed by a yelp, renewed again and again. Then, seemingly very far away, I heard a "Holloa! holloa!" as of many voices calling in unison. Cautiously I raised my head and looked in the direction whence the sound came; but the cemetery blocked my view. The wolf still continued to yelp in a strange way, and a red glare began to move round the grove of cypresses, as though following the sound. As the voices drew closer, the wolf yelped faster and louder. I feared to make either sound or motion.

Nearer came the red glow, over the white pall, which stretched into the darkness around me. Then all at once from beyond the trees there came at a trot a troop of horsemen bearing torches. The wolf rose from my breast and made for the cemetery. I saw one of the horsemen (soldiers by their caps and their long military cloaks) raise his carbine and take aim. A companion knocked up his arm, and I heard the ball whizz over my head. He had evidently taken my body for that of the wolf. Another sighted the animal as it slunk away, and a shot followed. Then, at a gallop, the troop rode forward — some towards me, others following the wolf as it disappeared amongst the snow-clad cypresses.

As they drew nearer, I tried to move, but was powerless, although I could see and hear all that went on around me. Two or three of the soldiers jumped from their horses and knelt beside me. One of them raised my head, and placed his hand over my heart.

"Good news, comrades!" he cried. "His heart still beats!"

Then some brandy was poured down my throat; it put vigor into me, and I was able to open my eyes fully and look around. Lights and shadows were moving among the trees, and I heard men call to one another. They drew together, uttering frightened exclamations; and the lights flashed as the others came pouring out of the cemetery pell-mell, like men possessed. When the further ones came close to us, those who were around me asked them eagerly:

"Well, have you found him?"

The reply rang out hurriedly:

"No! no! Come away quick — quick! This is no place to stay, and on this of all nights!"

"What was it?" was the question, asked in all manner of keys.

The answer came variously and all indefinitely as though the men were moved by some common impulse to speak, yet were restrained by some common fear from giving their thoughts.

"It—it—indeed!" gibbered one, whose wits had plainly given out for the moment.

"A wolf—and yet not a wolf!" another put in shudderingly.

"No use trying for him without the sacred bullet," a third remarked in a more ordinary manner.

"Serve us right for coming out on this night! Truly we have earned our thousand marks!" were the ejaculations of a fourth.

"There was blood on the broken marble," another said after a pause—"the lightning never brought that there. And for him—is he safe? Look at his throat! See, comrades, the wolf has been lying on him and keeping his blood warm."

The officer looked at my throat and replied:

"He is all right; the skin is not pierced. What does it all mean? We should never have found him but for the yelping of the wolf."

"What became of it?" asked the man who was holding up my head, and who seemed the least panic-stricken of the party, for his hands were steady and without tremor. On his sleeve was the chevron of a petty officer.

"It went to its home," answered the man, whose long face was pallid, and who actually shook with terror as he glanced around him fearfully. "There are graves enough there in which it may lie. Come, comrades—come quickly! Let us leave this cursed spot."

The officer raised me to a sitting posture, as he uttered a word of command; then several men placed me upon a horse. He sprang to the saddle behind me, took me in his arms, gave the word to advance; and, turning our faces away from the cypresses, we rode away in swift, military order.

As yet my tongue refused its office, and I was perforce silent. I must have fallen asleep; for the next thing I remembered was finding myself standing up, supported by a soldier on each side of me. It was almost broad daylight, and to the north a red streak of sunlight was reflected, like a path of blood, over the waste of snow. The officer was telling the men to say nothing of what they had seen, except that they found an English stranger, guarded by a large dog.

"Dog! that was no dog," cut in the man who had exhibited such fear. "I think I know a wolf when I see one."

The young officer answered calmly: "I said a dog."

"Dog!" reiterated the other ironically. It was evident that his courage was rising with the sun; and, pointing to me, he said, "Look at his throat. Is that the work of a dog, master?"

Instinctively I raised my hand to my throat, and as I touched it, I cried out in pain. The men crowded round to look, some stooping down from their saddles; and again there came the calm voice of the young officer:

"A dog, as I said. If aught else were said we should only be laughed at."

I was then mounted behind a trooper, and we rode on into the suburbs of Munich. Here we came across a stray carriage, into which I was lifted, and it was driven off to the Quatre Saisons — the young officer accompanying me, whilst a trooper followed with his horse, and the others rode off to their barracks.

When we arrived, Herr Delbrück rushed so quickly down the steps to meet me, that it was apparent he had been watching within. Taking me by both hands he solicitously led me in. The officer saluted me and was turning to withdraw, when I recognized his purpose, and insisted that he should come to my rooms. Over a glass of wine, I warmly thanked him and his brave comrades for saving me. He replied simply that he was more than glad, and that Herr Delbrück had at the first taken steps to make all the searching party pleased; at which ambiguous utterance the *maître d'hôtel* smiled, while the officer pleaded duty and withdrew.

"But Herr Delbrück," I enquired, "how and why was it that the soldiers searched for me?"

He shrugged his shoulders, as if in depreciation of his own deed, as he replied:

"I was so fortunate as to obtain leave from the commander of the regiment in which I served, to ask for volunteers."

"But how did you know I was lost?" I asked.

"The driver came hither with the remains of his carriage, which had been upset when the horses ran away."

"But surely you would not send a search-party of soldiers merely on this account?"

"Oh, no!" he answered; "but even before the coachman arrived, I had this telegram from the Boyar whose guest you are," and he took from his pocket a telegram which he handed to me, and I read:

BISTRITZ

Be careful of my guest—his safety is most precious to me. Should aught happen to him, or if he be missed, spare nothing to find him and ensure his safety. He is English and therefore adventurous. There are often dangers from snow and wolves and night. Lose not a moment if you suspect harm to him. I answer your zeal with my fortune.—Dracula

As I held the telegram in my hand, the room seemed to whirl

around me; and, if the attentive *maître d'hôtel* had not caught me, I think I should have fallen. There was something so strange in all this, something so weird and impossible to imagine, that there grew on me a sense of my being in some way the sport of opposite forces—the mere vague idea of which seemed in a way to paralyze me. I was certainly under some form of mysterious protection. From a distant country had come, in the very nick of time, a message that took me out of the danger of the snow-sleep and the jaws of the wolf.

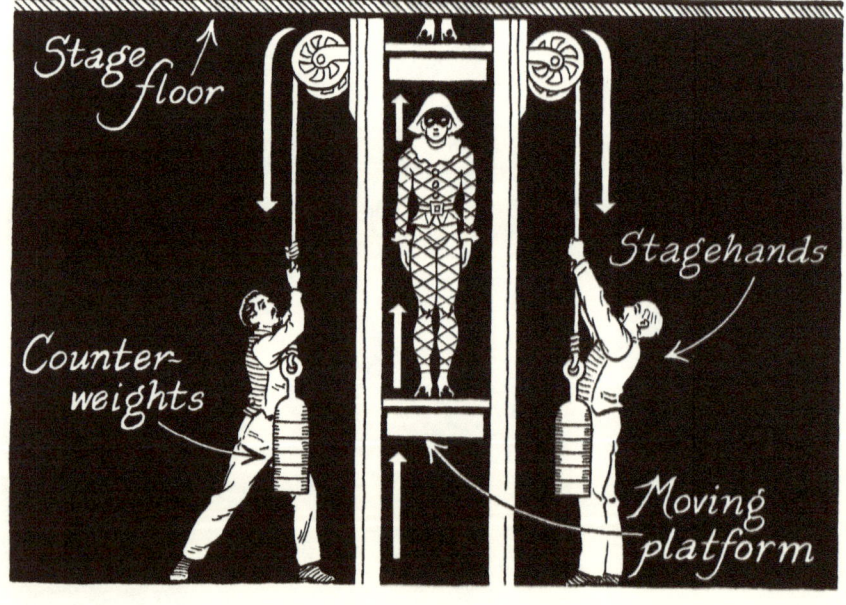

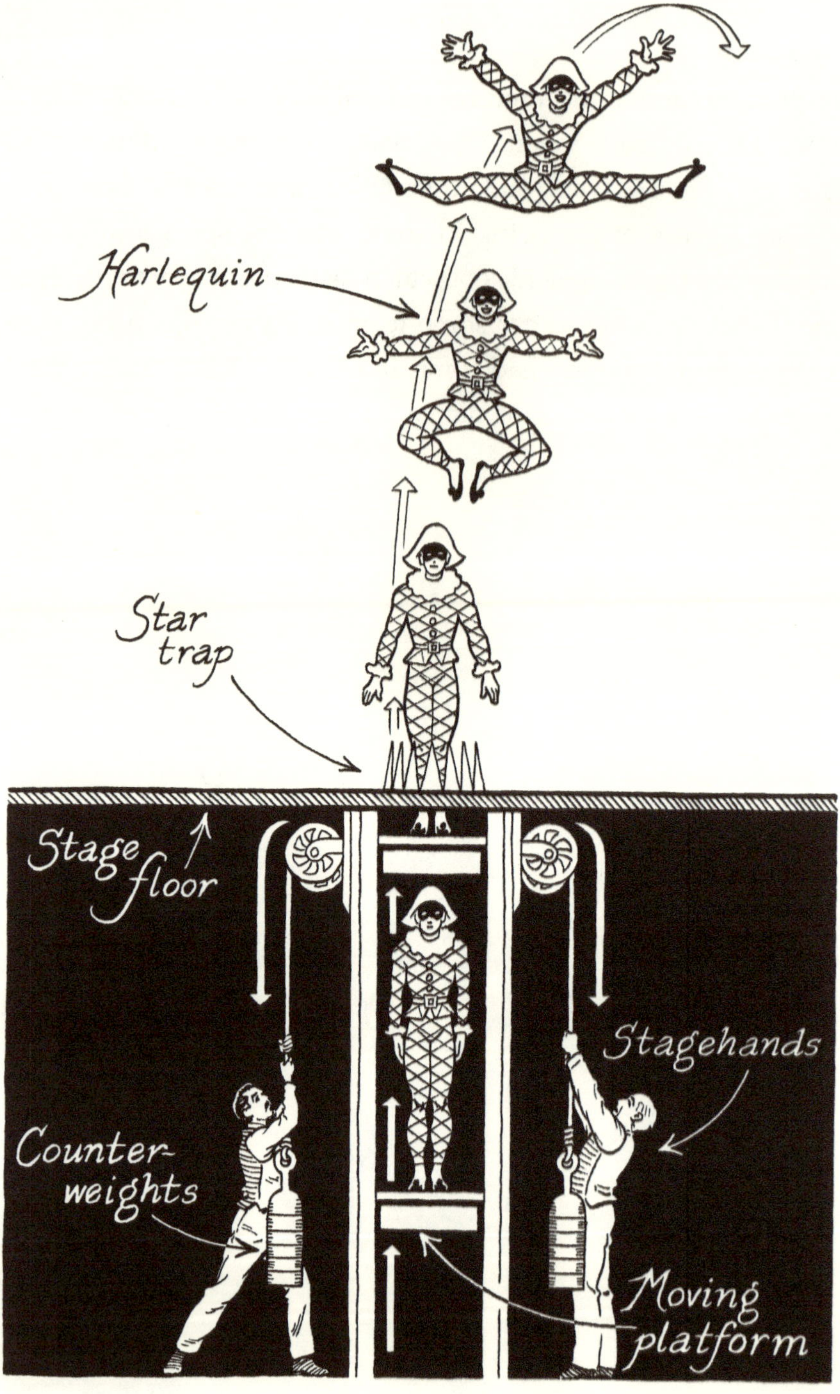

Harlequin

Star trap

Stage floor

Stagehands

Counter-weights

Moving platform

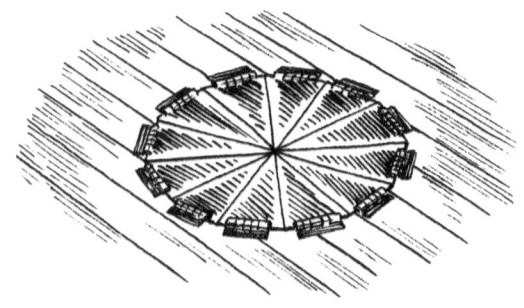

A STAR TRAP

WHEN I WAS APPRENTICED to theatrical carpentering my master was John Haliday, who was Master Machinist — we called men in his post "Master Carpenter" in those days — of the old Victoria Theatre, Hulme. It wasn't called Hulme; but that name will do. It would only stir up painful memories if I were to give the real name. I daresay some of you — not the Ladies (this with a gallant bow all round) — will remember the case of a Harlequin as was killed in an accident in the pantomime. We needn't mention names; Mortimer will do for a name to call him by — Henry Mortimer. The cause of it was never found out. But I knew it; and I've kept silence for so long that I may speak now without hurting anyone. They're all dead long ago that was interested in the death of Henry Mortimer or the man who wrought that death.

Any of you who know of the case will remember what a handsome, dapper, well-built man Mortimer was. To my own mind he was the handsomest man I ever saw.

Of course, I was only a boy then, and I hadn't seen any of you gentlemen. I needn't tell you, Ladies, how well a harlequin's dress sets off a nice slim figure. No wonder that in these days of suffragettes, women wants to be harlequins as well as columbines. Though I hope they won't make the columbine a man's part!

Mortimer was the nimblest chap at the traps I ever see. He was so sure of hisself that he would have extra weight put on so that when the counter weights fell, he'd shoot up five or six feet higher than anyone else could even try to. Moreover, he had a way of drawing up his legs when in the air — the way a frog does when he is swimming — that made his jump look ever so much higher.

I think the girls were all in love with him, the way they used to stand in the wings when the time was comin' for his entrance. That wouldn't have mattered much, for girls are always falling in love with some man or other, but it made trouble, as it always does when the married ones take the same start. There were several of these that were always after him, more shame for them, with husbands of their own. That was dangerous enough, and hard to stand for a man who might mean to be decent in any way. But the real trial — and the real trouble, too — was none other than the young wife of my own master, and she was more than flesh and blood could stand. She had come into the panto, the season before, as a high-kicker — and she could! She could kick higher than girls that was more than a foot taller than her; for she was a wee bit of a thing and as pretty as pie; a gold-haired, blue-eyed, slim thing with much the figure of a boy, except for. . . and they saved her from any mistaken idea of that kind. Jack Haliday went crazy over her, and when the notice was up, and there was no young spark with plenty of oof coming along to do the proper thing by her, she married him. It was, when they was joined, what you Ladies call a marriage of convenience; but after a bit they two got on very well, and we all thought she was beginning to like the old man—for Jack was old enough to be her father, with a bit to spare. In the summer, when the house was closed, he took her to the Isle of Man; and when they came back, he made no secret of it that he'd had the happiest time of his life. She looked quite happy, too, and treated him affectionate; and we all began to think that that marriage had not been a failure at any rate.

Things began to change, however, when the panto rehearsals began next year. Old Jack began to look unhappy, and didn't take no interest in his work. Loo—that was Mrs. Haliday's name—didn't seem over fond of him now, and was generally impatient when he was by. Nobody said anything about this, however, to us men; but the married women smiled and nodded their heads and whispered that perhaps there were reasons. One day on the stage, when the harlequinade rehearsal was beginning, someone mentioned as how perhaps Mrs. Haliday wouldn't be dancing that year, and they smiled as if they was all in the secret. Then Mrs. Jack ups and gives them Johnny-up-the-orchard for not minding their own business and telling a pack of lies, and such like as you Ladies like to express in your own ways when you get your back hair down. The rest of us tried to soothe her all we could, and she went off home.

It wasn't long after that that she and Henry Mortimer left together after rehearsal was over, he saying he'd leave her at home. She didn't make no objections—I told you he was a very handsome man.

Well, from that on she never seemed to take her eyes from him during every rehearsal, right up to the night of the last rehearsal, which, of course, was full dress — "Everybody and Everything."

Jack Haliday never seemed to notice anything that was going on, like the rest of them did. True, his time was taken up with his own work, for I'm telling you that a Master Machinist hasn't got no loose time on his hands at the first dress rehearsal of a panto. And, of course, none of the company ever said a word or gave a look that would call his attention to it. Men and women are queer beings. They will be blind and deaf whilst danger is being run; and it's only after the scandal is beyond repair that they begin to talk — just the very time when most of all they should be silent.

I saw all that went on, but I didn't understand it. I liked Mortimer myself and admired him — like I did Mrs. Haliday, too — and I thought he was a very fine fellow. I was only a boy, you know, and Haliday's apprentice, so naturally I wasn't looking for any trouble I could help, even if I'd seen it coming. It was when I looked back afterwards at the whole thing that I began to comprehend; so you will all understand now, I hope, that what I tell you is the result of much knowledge of what I saw and heard and was told of afterwards — all morticed and clamped up by thinking.

The panto had been on about three weeks when one Saturday, between the shows, I heard two of our company talking. Both of them was among the extra girls that both sang and danced and had to make theirselves useful. I don't think either of them was better than she should be; they went out to too many champagne suppers with young men that had money to burn. That part doesn't matter in this affair — except that they was naturally enough jealous of women who was married — which was what they was aiming at — and what lived straighter than they did. Women of that kind like to see a good woman tumble down; it seems to make them all more even. Now real bad girls what have gone under altogether will try to save a decent one from following their road. That is, so long as they're young; for a bad one what is long in the tooth is the limit. They'll help anyone down hill—so long as they get anything out of it.

Well—no offence, you Ladies, as has growed up!—these two girls was enjoyin' themselves over Mrs. Haliday and the mash she had set up on Mortimer. They didn't see that I was sitting on a stage box behind a built-out piece of the Prologue of the panto, which was set ready for night. They were both in love with Mortimer, who wouldn't look at either of them, so they was miaw'n cruel, like cats on the tiles. Says one:

"The Old Man seems worse than blind; he won't see."

"Don't you be too sure of that," says the other. "He don't mean to take no chances. I think you must be blind, too, Kissie." That was her name—on the bills anyhow, Kissie Mountpelier. "Don't he make a point of taking her home hisself every night after the play. You should know, for you're in the hall yourself waiting for your young man till he comes from his club."

"Wot-ho, you bally geeser," says the other—which her language was mostly coarse—"don't you know there's two ends to everything? The Old Man looks to one end only!" Then they began to snigger and whisper; and presently the other one says:

"Then he thinks harm can be only done when work is over!"

"Jest so," she answers. "Her and him knows that the old man has to be down long before the risin' of the rag; but she doesn't come in till the Vision of Venus dance after half time; and he not till the harlequinade!"

Then I quit. I didn't want to hear any more of that sort.

All that week things went on as usual. Poor old Haliday wasn't well. He looked worried and had a devil of a temper. I had reason to know that, for what worried him was his work. He was always a hard worker, and the panto season was a terror with him. He didn't ever seem to mind anything else outside his work. I thought at the time that that was how those two chattering girls made up their slanderous story; for, after all, a slander, no matter how false it may be, must have some sort of beginning. Something that seems, if there isn't something that is! But no matter how busy he might be, old Jack always made time to leave the wife at home.

As the week went on, he got more and more pale; and I began to think he was in for some sickness. He generally remained in the theatre between the shows on Saturday; that is, he didn't go home, but took a high tea in the coffee shop close to the theatre, so as to be handy in case there might be a hitch anywhere in the preparation for night. On that Saturday he went out as usual when the first scene was set, and the men were getting ready the packs for the rest of the scenes. By and bye there was some trouble — the usual Saturday kind — and I went off to tell him. When I went into the coffee shop, I couldn't see him. I thought it best not to ask or to seem to take any notice, so I came back to the theatre and heard that the trouble had settled itself, as usual, by the men who had been quarrelling going off to have another drink. I hustled up those who remained, and we got things smoothed out in time for them all to have their tea. Then I had my own. I was just then beginning to feel the responsibility of my business, so I wasn't long over my food, but came back to look things over and see that all was right, especially the trap, for that was a thing Jack Haliday was most particular about. He would overlook a fault for anything else; but if it was along of a trap, the man had to go. He always told the men that that wasn't ordinary work; it was life or death.

I had just got through my inspection when I saw old Jack coming in from the hall. There was no one about at that hour, and the stage was dark. But dark as it was, I could see that the old man was ghastly pale. I didn't speak, for I wasn't near enough, and as he was moving very silently behind the scenes, I thought that perhaps he wouldn't like anyone to notice that he had been away. I thought the best thing I could do would be to clear out of the way, so I went back and had another cup of tea.

I came away a little before the men, who had nothing to think of except to be in their places when Haliday's whistle sounded. I went to report myself to my master, who was in his own little glass-partitioned den at the back of the carpenter's shop. He was there bent over his own bench, and was filing away at something so intently that he did not seem to hear me; so I cleared out. I tell you, Ladies and Gents, that from an apprentice point of view it is not wise to be too obtrusive when your master is attending to some private matter of his own!

When the "get-ready" time came and the lights went up, there was Haliday as usual at his post. He looked very white and ill—so ill that the stage manager, when he came in, said to him that if he liked to go home and rest, he would see that all his work would be attended to. He thanked him, and said that he thought he would be able to stay. "I do feel a little weak and ill, sir," he said. "I felt just now for a few moments as if I was going to faint. But that's gone by already, and I'm sure I shall be able to get through the work before us all right."

Then the doors was opened, and the Saturday night audience came rushing and tumbling in. The Victoria was a great Saturday night house. No matter what other nights might be, that was sure to be good. They used to say in the perfesh that the Victoria lived on it, and that the management was on holiday for the rest of the week. The actors knew it, and no matter how slack they might be from Monday to Friday they was all taut and trim then. There was no walking through and no fluffing on Saturday nights — or else they'd have had the bird.

Mortimer was one of the most particular of the lot in this way. He never was slack at any time — indeed, slackness is not a harlequin's fault, for if there's slackness there's no harlequin, that's all. But Mortimer always put on an extra bit on the Saturday night. When he jumped up through the star trap, he always went then a couple of feet higher. To do this we had always to put on a lot more weight. This he always saw to himself; for, mind you, it's no joke being driven up through the trap as if you was shot out of a gun. The points of the star had to be kept free, and the hinges at their bases must be well oiled, or else there can be a disaster at any time. Moreover, 'tis the duty of someone appointed for the purpose to see that all is clear upon the stage. I remember hearing that once at New York, many years ago now, a harlequin was killed by a "grip" — as the Yankees call a carpenter — what outsiders here call a scene-shifter — walking over the trap just as the stroke had been given to let go the counter-weights. It wasn't much satisfaction to the widow to know that the "grip" was killed too.

That night Mrs. Haliday looked prettier than ever, and kicked even higher than I had ever seen her do. Then, when she got dressed for home, she came as usual and stood in the wings for the beginning of the harlequinade. Old Jack came across the stage and stood beside her; I saw him from the back follow up the sliding ground-row that closed in on the Realms of Delight. I couldn't help noticing that he still looked ghastly pale. He kept turning his eyes on the star trap. Seeing this, I naturally looked at it too, for I feared lest something might have gone wrong. I had seen that it was in good order, and that the joints were properly oiled when the stage was set for the evening show, and as it wasn't used all night for anything else I was reassured. Indeed, I thought I could see it shine a bit as the limelight caught the brass hinges. There was a spotlight just above it on the bridge, which was intended to make a good show of harlequin and his big jump. The people used to howl with delight as he came rushing up through the trap and when in the air drew up his legs and spread them wide for an instant and then straightened them again as he came down—only bending his knees just as he touched the stage.

When the signal was given, the counter-weight worked properly. I knew, for the sound of it at that part was all right.

But something was wrong. The trap didn't work smooth, and open at once as the harlequin's head touched it. There was a shock and a tearing sound, and the pieces of the star seemed torn about, and some of them were thrown about the stage. And in the middle of them came the colored and spangled figure that we knew.

But somehow it didn't come up in the usual way. It was erect enough, but there was not the usual elasticity. The legs never moved; and when it went up a fair height—though nothing like usual—it seemed to topple over and fall on the stage on its side. The audience shrieked, and the people in the wings—actors and staff all the same—closed in, some of them in their stage clothes, others dressed for going home. But the man in the spangles lay quite still.

The loudest shriek of all was from Mrs. Haliday; and she was the first to reach the spot where he — it — lay. Old Jack was close behind her and caught her as she fell. I had just time to see that, for I made it my business to look after the pieces of the trap; there was plenty of people to look after the corpse. And the pit was by now crossing the orchestra and climbing up on the stage.

I managed to get the bits together before the rush came. I noticed that there were deep scratches on some of them, but I didn't have time for more than a glance. I put a stage box over the hole lest anyone should put a foot through it. Such would mean a broken leg at least; and if one fell through, it might mean worse. Amongst other things I found a queer-looking piece of flat steel with some bent points on it. I knew it didn't belong to the trap; but it came from somewhere, so I put it in my pocket.

By this time there was a crowd where Mortimer's body lay. That he was stone dead nobody could doubt. The very attitude was enough. He was all straggled about in queer positions; one of the legs was doubled under him with the toes sticking out in the wrong way. But let that suffice! It doesn't do to go into details of a dead body . . . I wish someone would give me a drop of punch.

There was another crowd round Mrs. Haliday, who was lying a little on one side nearer the wings where her husband had carried her and laid her down. She, too, looked like a corpse; for she was as white as one and as still, and looked as cold. Old Jack was kneeling beside her, chafing her hands. He was evidently frightened about her, for he, too, was deathly white. However, he kept his head, and called his men round him. He left his wife in care of Mrs.

Homcroft, the Wardrobe Mistress, who had by this time hurried down. She was a capable woman, and knew how to act promptly. She got one of the men to lift Mrs. Haliday and carry her up to the wardrobe. I heard afterwards that when she got her there, she turned out all the rest of them that followed up—the women as well as the men—and looked after her herself.

I put the pieces of the broken trap on the top of the stage box, and told one of our chaps to mind them and see that no one touched them, as they might be wanted. By this time the police who had been on duty in front had come round, and as they had at once telephoned to headquarters, more police kept coming in all the time. One of them took charge of the place where the broken trap was; and when he heard who put the box and the broken pieces there, sent for me. More of them took the body away to the property room, which was a large room with benches in it, and which could be locked up. Two of them stood at the door and wouldn't let anyone go in without permission.

The man who was in charge of the trap asked me if I had seen the accident. When I said I had, he asked me to describe it. I don't think he had much opinion of my powers of description, for he soon dropped that part of his questioning. Then he asked me to point out where I found the bits of the broken trap. I simply said:

"Lord bless you, sir, I couldn't tell. They was scattered all over the place. I had to pick them up between people's feet as they were rushing in from all sides."

"All right, my boy," he said, in quite a kindly way, for a policeman, "I don't think they'll want to worry you. There are lots of men and women, I am told, who were standing by and saw the whole thing. They will be all subpoenaed." I was a small-made lad in those days — I ain't a giant now! — and I suppose he thought it was no use having children for witnesses when they had plenty of grown-ups. Then he said something about me and an idiot asylum that was not kind — no, nor wise either, for I dried up and did not say another word.

Gradually the public was got rid of. Some strolled off by degrees, going off to have a glass before the pubs closed, and talk it all over. The rest us and the police ballooned out. Then, when the police had taken charge of everything and put in men to stay all night, the coroner's officer came and took off the body to the city mortuary, where the police doctor made a post mortem. I was allowed to go home. I did so — and gladly — when I had seen the place settling down. Mr. Haliday took his wife home in a four-wheeler. It was perhaps just as well, for Mrs. Homcroft and some other kindly souls had poured so much whisky and brandy and rum and gin and beer and peppermint into her that I don't believe she could have walked if she had tried.

When I was undressing myself, something scratched my leg as I was taking off my trousers. I found it was the piece of flat steel, which I had picked up on the stage. It was in the shape of a star fish, but the spikes of it were short. Some of the points were turned down, the rest were pulled out straight again. I stood with it in my hand wondering where it had come from and what it was for, but I couldn't remember anything in the whole theatre that it could have belonged to. I looked at it closely again, and saw that the edges were all filed and quite bright. But that did not help me, so I put it on the table and thought I would take it with me in the morning; perhaps one of the chaps might know. I turned out the gas and went to bed — and to sleep.

I must have begun to dream at once, and it was, naturally enough, all about the terrible thing that had occurred. But, like all dreams, it was a bit mixed. They were all mixed. Mortimer with his spangles flying up the trap, it breaking, and the pieces scattering round. Old Jack Haliday looking on at one side of the stage with his wife beside him—he as pale as death, and she looking prettier than ever. And then Mortimer coming down all crooked and falling on the stage, Mrs. Haliday shrieking, and her and Jack running forward, and me picking up the pieces of the broken trap from between people's legs, and finding the steel star with the bent points.

I woke in a cold sweat, saying to myself as I sat up in bed in the dark:

"That's it!"

And then my head began to reel about so that I lay down again and began to think it all over. And it all seemed clear enough then. It was Mr. Haliday who made that star and put it over the star trap where the points joined! That was what Jack Haliday was filing at when I saw him at his bench; and he had done it because Mortimer and his wife had been making love to each other. Those girls were right, after all. Of course, the steel points had prevented the trap opening, and when Mortimer was driven up against it his neck was broken.

But then came the horrible thought that if Jack did it, it was murder, and he would be hung. And, after all, it was his wife that the harlequin had made love to—and old Jack loved her very much indeed himself and had been good to her—and she was his wife. And that bit of steel would hang him if it should be known. But no one but me—and whoever made it, and put it on the trap—even knew of its existence — and Mr. Haliday was my master — and the man was dead — and he was a villain!

I was living then at Quarry Place; and in the old quarry was a pond so deep that the boys used to say that far down the water was boiling hot, it was so near Hell.

I softly opened the window, and, there in the dark, threw the bit of steel as far as I could into the quarry.

No one ever knew, for I have never spoken a word of it till this very minute. I was not called at the inquest. Everyone was in a hurry; the coroner and the jury and the police. Our governor was in a hurry too, because we wanted to go on as usual at night; and too much talk of the tragedy would hurt business. So nothing was known; and all went on as usual. Except that after that, Mrs. Haliday didn't stand in the wings during the harlequinade, and she was as loving to her old husband as a woman can be. It was him she used to watch now; and always with a sort of respectful adoration. She knew, though no one else did, except her husband — and me.

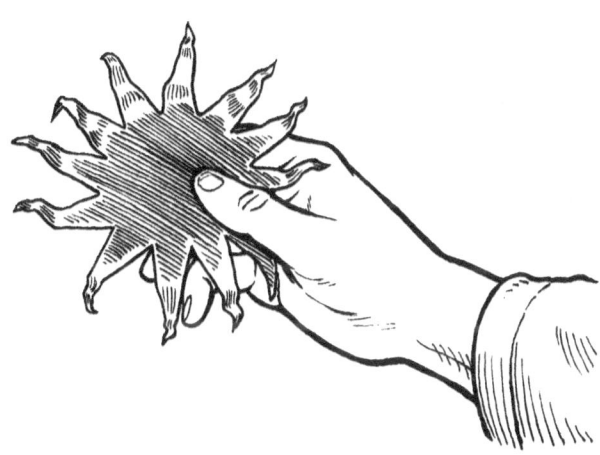

THE JUDGE'S HOUSE

WHEN THE TIME for his examination drew near, Malcolm Malcolmson made up his mind to go somewhere to read by himself. He feared the attractions of the seaside, and also he feared completely rural isolation, for of old he knew its charms, and so he determined to find some unpretentious little town where there would be nothing to distract him. He refrained from asking suggestions from any of his friends, for he argued that each would recommend some place of which he had knowledge and where he had already acquaintances. As Malcolmson wished to avoid friends, he had no wish to encumber himself with the attention of friends' friends, and so he determined to look out for a place for himself. He packed a portmanteau with some clothes and all the books he required and then took ticket for the first name on the local timetable which he did not know.

When at the end of three hours' journey he alighted at Ben-church, he felt satisfied that he had so far obliterated his tracks as to be sure of having a peaceful opportunity of pursuing his studies. He went straight to the one inn which the sleepy little place contained, and put up for the night. Benchurch was a market town, and once in three weeks was crowded to excess, but for the remainder of the twenty-one days it was as attractive as a desert. Malcolmson looked around the day after his arrival to try to find quarters more isolated than even so quiet an inn as "The Good Traveller" afforded. There was only one place which took his fancy, and it certainly satisfied his wildest ideas regarding quiet; in fact, quiet was not the proper word to apply to it—desolation was the only term conveying any suitable idea of its isolation. It was an old rambling, heavy-built house of the Jacobean style, with heavy gables and windows, unusually small, and set higher than was customary in such houses, and was surrounded with a high brick wall massively built. Indeed, on examination, it looked more like a fortified house than an ordinary dwelling. But all these things pleased Malcolmson. "Here," he thought, "is the very spot I have been looking for, and if I can get opportunity of using it, I shall be happy." His joy was increased when he realized beyond doubt that it was not at present inhabited.

From the post-office he got the name of the agent, who was rarely surprised at the application to rent a part of the old house. Mr. Carnford, the local lawyer and agent, was a genial old gentleman, and frankly confessed his delight at anyone being willing to live in the house.

"To tell you the truth," said he, "I should be only too happy, on behalf of the owners, to let anyone have the house rent free for a term of years if only to accustom the people here to see it inhabited. It has been so long empty that some kind of absurd prejudice has grown up about it, and this can be best put down by its occupation—if only," he added with a sly glance at Malcolmson, "by a scholar like yourself, who wants its quiet for a time."

Malcolmson thought it needless to ask the agent about the "absurd prejudice"; he knew he would get more information, if he should require it, on that subject from other quarters. He paid his three months' rent, got a receipt, and the name of an old woman who would probably undertake to "do" for him, and came away with the keys in his pocket. He then went to the landlady of the inn, who was a cheerful and most kindly person, and asked her advice as to such stores and provisions as he would be likely to require. She threw up her hands in amazement when he told her where he was going to settle himself.

"Not in the Judge's House!" she said, and grew pale as she spoke. He explained the locality of the house, saying that he did not know its name. When he had finished, she answered:

"Aye, sure enough—sure enough the very place! It is the Judge's House sure enough." He asked her to tell him about the place, why so called, and what there was against it. She told him that it was so called locally because it had been many years before— how long she could not say, as she was herself from another part of the country, but she thought it must have been a hundred years or more—the abode of a judge who was held in great terror on account of his harsh sentences and his hostility to prisoners at Assizes. As to what there was against the house itself, she could not tell. She had often asked, but no one could inform her; but there was a general feeling that there was *something*, and for her own part she

would not take all the money in Drinkwater's Bank and stay in the house an hour by herself. Then she apologized to Malcolmson for her disturbing talk.

"It is too bad of me, sir, and you—and a young gentlemen, too—if you will pardon me saying it, going to live there all alone. If you were my boy—and you'll excuse me for saying it—you wouldn't sleep there a night, not if I had to go there myself and pull the big alarm bell that's on the roof!" The good creature was so manifestly in earnest, and was so kindly in her intentions, that Malcolmson, although amused, was touched. He told her kindly how much he appreciated her interest in him, and added:

"But, my dear Mrs. Witham, indeed you need not be concerned about me! A man who is reading for the Mathematical Tripos has too much to think of to be disturbed by any of these mysterious 'somethings,' and his work is of too exact and prosaic a kind to allow of his having any corner in his mind for mysteries of any kind. Harmonical Progression, Permutations and Combinations, and Elliptic Functions have sufficient mysteries for me!" Mrs. Witham kindly undertook to see after his commissions, and he went himself to look for the old woman who had been recommended to him. When he returned to the Judge's House with her, after an interval of a couple of hours, he found Mrs. Witham herself waiting with several men and boys carrying parcels, and an upholsterer's man with a bed in a car, for she said, though tables and chairs might be all very well, a bed that hadn't been aired for mayhap fifty years was not proper for young bones to lie on. She was evidently curious to see the inside of the house; and though manifestly so afraid of the "somethings" that at the slightest sound she clutched on to Malcolmson, whom she never left for a moment, went over the whole place.

After his examination of the house, Malcolmson decided to take up his abode in the great dining-room, which was big enough to serve for all his requirements; and Mrs. Witham, with the aid of the charwoman, Mrs. Dempster, proceeded to arrange matters. When the hampers were brought in and unpacked, Malcolmson saw that with much kind forethought she had sent from her own kitchen sufficient provisions to last for a few days. Before going she expressed all sorts of kind wishes; and at the door turned and said:

"And perhaps, sir, as the room is big and draughty it might be well to have one of those big screens put round your bed at night — though, truth to tell, I would die myself if I were to be so shut in with all kinds of — of 'things', that put their heads round the sides, or over the top, and look on me!" The image which she had called up was too much for her nerves, and she fled incontinently.

Mrs. Dempster sniffed in a superior manner as the landlady disappeared, and remarked that for her own part she wasn't afraid of all the bogies in the kingdom.

"I'll tell you what it is, sir," she said; "bogies is all kinds and sorts of things — except bogies! Rats and mice, and beetles; and creaky doors, and loose slates, and broken panes, and stiff drawer handles, that stay out when you pull them and then fall down in the middle of the night. Look at the wainscot of the room! It is old — hundreds of years old! Do you think there's no rats and beetles there! And do you imagine, sir, that you won't see none of them? Rats is bogies, I tell you, and bogies is rats; and don't you get to think anything else!"

"Mrs. Dempster," said Malcolmson gravely, making her a polite bow, "you know more than a Senior Wrangler! And let me say, that, as a mark of esteem for your indubitable soundness of head and heart, I shall, when I go, give you possession of this house, and let

you stay here by yourself for the last two months of my tenancy, for four weeks will serve my purpose."

"Thank you kindly, sir!" she answered, "but I couldn't sleep away from home a night. I am in Greenhow's Charity, and if I slept a night away from my rooms, I should lose all I have got to live on. The rules is very strict; and there's too many watching for a vacancy for me to run any risks in the matter. Only for that, sir, I'd gladly come here and attend on you altogether during your stay."

"My good woman," said Malcolmson hastily, "I have come here on purpose to obtain solitude; and believe me that I am grateful to the late Greenhow for having so organized his admirable charity — whatever it is — that I am perforce denied the opportunity of suffering from such a form of temptation! Saint Anthony himself could not be more rigid on the point!"

The old woman laughed harshly. "Ah, you young gentlemen," she said, "you don't fear for naught; and belike you'll get all the solitude you want here." She set to work with her cleaning; and by nightfall, when Malcolmson returned from his walk — he always had one of his books to study as he walked — he found the room swept and tidied, a fire burning in the old hearth, the lamp lit, and the table spread for supper with Mrs. Witham's excellent fare. "This is comfort, indeed," he said, as he rubbed his hands.

When he had finished his supper and lifted the tray to the other end of the great oak dining-table, he got out his books again, put fresh wood on the fire, trimmed his lamp, and set himself down to a spell of real hard work. He went on without pause till about eleven o'clock, when he knocked off for a bit to fix his fire and lamp, and to make himself a cup of tea. He had always been a tea-drinker, and during his college life had sat late at work and had taken tea late. The rest was a great luxury to him, and he enjoyed it with a sense of delicious, voluptuous ease. The renewed fire leaped and sparkled, and threw quaint shadows through the great old room; and as he sipped his hot tea he reveled in the sense of isolation from his kind. Then it was that he began to notice for the first time what a noise the rats were making.

"Surely," he thought, "they cannot have been at it all the time I was reading. Had they been, I must have noticed it!" Presently, when the noise increased, he satisfied himself that it was really new. It was evident that at first the rats had been frightened at the presence of a stranger, and the light of fire and lamp; but that as the time went on, they had grown bolder and were now disporting themselves as was their wont.

How busy they were! and hark to the strange noises! Up and down behind the old wainscot, over the ceiling and under the floor they raced, and gnawed, and scratched! Malcolmson smiled to himself as he recalled to mind the saying of Mrs. Dempster, "Bogies is rats, and rats is bogies!" The tea began to have its effect of intellectual and nervous stimulus, he saw with joy another long spell of work to be done before the night was past, and in the sense of security which it gave him, he allowed himself the luxury of a good look round the room. He took his lamp in one hand, and went all around, wondering that so quaint and beautiful an old house had been so long neglected. The carving of the oak on the panels of the wainscot was fine, and on and round the doors and windows it was beautiful and of rare merit. There were some old pictures on the walls, but they were coated so thick with dust and dirt that he could not distinguish any detail of them, though he held his lamp as high as he could over his head. Here and there as he went round, he saw some crack or hole

blocked for a moment by the face of a rat with its bright eyes glittering in the light, but in an instant, it was gone, and a squeak and a scamper followed. The thing that most struck him, however, was the rope of the great alarm bell on the roof, which hung down in a corner of the room on the right-hand side of the fireplace. He pulled up close to the hearth a great high-backed carved oak chair, and sat down to his last cup of tea. When this was done, he made up the fire, and went back to his work, sitting at the corner of the table, having the fire to his left. For a little while the rats disturbed him somewhat with their perpetual scampering, but he got accustomed to the noise as one does to the ticking of a clock or to the roar of moving water; and he became so immersed in his work that everything in the world, except the problem which he was trying to solve, passed away from him.

He suddenly looked up, his problem was still unsolved, and there was in the air that sense of the hour before the dawn, which is so dread to doubtful life. The noise of the rats had ceased. Indeed, it seemed to him that it must have ceased but lately and that it was the sudden cessation which had disturbed him. The fire had fallen low, but still it threw out a deep red glow. As he looked, he started in spite of his *sang froid*.

There on the great high-backed carved oak chair by the right side of the fireplace sat an enormous rat, steadily glaring at him with baleful eyes. He made a motion to it as though to hunt it away, but it did not stir. Then he made the motion of throwing something. Still it did not stir, but showed its great white teeth angrily, and its cruel eyes shone in the lamplight with an added vindictiveness.

Malcolmson felt amazed, and seizing the poker from the hearth ran at it to kill it. Before, however, he could strike it, the rat, with a squeak that sounded like the concentration of hate, jumped upon the floor, and, running up the rope of the alarm bell, disappeared in the darkness beyond the range of the green-shaded lamp. Instantly, strange to say, the noisy scampering of the rats in the wainscot began again.

By this time Malcolmson's mind was quite off the problem; and as a shrill cock-crow outside told him of the approach of morning, he went to bed and to sleep.

He slept so sound that he was not even waked by Mrs. Dempster coming in to make up his room. It was only when she had tidied up the place and got his breakfast ready and tapped on the screen which closed in his bed that he woke. He was a little tired still after his night's hard work, but a strong cup of tea soon freshened him up and, taking his book, he went out for his morning walk, bringing with him a few sandwiches lest he should not care to return till dinner time. He found a quiet walk between high elms some way outside the town, and here he spent the greater part of the day studying his Laplace. On his return he looked in to see Mrs. Witham and to thank her for her kindness. When she saw him coming through the diamond-paned bay window of her sanctum, she came out to meet him and asked him in. She looked at him searchingly and shook her head as she said:

"You must not overdo it, sir. You are paler this morning than you should be. Too late hours and too hard work on the brain isn't good for any man! But tell me, sir, how did you pass the night? Well, I hope? But my heart! sir, I was glad when Mrs. Dempster told me this morning that you were all right and sleeping sound when she went in."

"Oh, I was all right," he answered smiling, "the 'somethings' didn't worry me, as yet. Only the rats; and they had a circus, I tell

you, all over the place. There was one wicked looking old devil that sat up on my own chair by the fire, and wouldn't go till I took the poker to him, and then he ran up the rope of the alarm bell and got to somewhere up the wall or the ceiling—I couldn't see where, it was so dark."

"Mercy on us," said Mrs. Witham, "an old devil, and sitting on a chair by the fireside! Take care, sir! take care! There's many a true word spoken in jest."

"How do you mean? 'Pon my word I don't understand."

"An old devil! The old devil, perhaps. There! sir, you needn't laugh," for Malcolmson had broken into a hearty peal. "You young folks thinks it easy to laugh at things that makes older ones shudder. Never mind, sir! never mind! Please God, you'll laugh all the time. It's what I wish you myself!" and the good lady beamed all over in sympathy with his enjoyment, her fears gone for a moment.

"Oh, forgive me!" said Malcolmson presently. "Don't think me rude; but the idea was too much for me—that the old devil himself was on the chair last night!" And at the thought he laughed again. Then he went home to dinner.

This evening the scampering of the rats began earlier; indeed it had been going on before his arrival, and only ceased whilst his presence by its freshness disturbed them. After dinner he sat by the fire for a while and had a smoke; and then, having cleared his table, began to work as before. Tonight the rats disturbed him more than they had done on the previous night. How they scampered up and down and under and over! How they squeaked, and scratched, and gnawed! How they, getting bolder by degrees, came to the mouths of their holes and to the chinks and cracks and crannies in the wainscoting till their eyes shone like tiny lamps as the firelight rose and fell. But to him, now doubtless accustomed to them, their eyes were not wicked; only their playfulness touched him. Sometimes the boldest of them made sallies out on the floor or along the mouldings of the wainscot. Now and again as they disturbed him Malcolmson made a sound to frighten them, smiting the table with his hand or giving a fierce "Hsh, hsh," so that they fled straightway to their holes.

And so the early part of the night wore on; and despite the noise Malcolmson got more and more immersed in his work.

All at once he stopped, as on the previous night, being overcome by a sudden sense of silence. There was not the faintest sound of gnaw, or scratch, or squeak. The silence was as of the grave. He remembered the odd occurrence of the previous night, and instinctively he looked at the chair standing close by the fireside. And then a very odd sensation thrilled through him.

There, on the great old high-backed carved oak chair beside the fireplace sat the same enormous rat, steadily glaring at him with baleful eyes.

Instinctively he took the nearest thing to his hand, a book of logarithms, and flung it at it. The book was badly aimed and the rat did not stir, so again the poker performance of the previous night was repeated; and again the rat, being closely pursued, fled up the rope of the alarm bell. Strangely too, the departure of this rat was instantly followed by the renewal of the noise made by the general rat community. On this occasion, as on the previous one, Malcolmson could not see at what part of the room the rat disappeared, for the green shade of his lamp left the upper part of the room in darkness, and the fire had burned low.

On looking at his watch he found it was close on midnight; and, not sorry for the *divertissement*, he made up his fire and made himself his nightly pot of tea. He had got through a good spell of work, and thought himself entitled to a cigarette; and so he sat on the great oak chair before the fire and enjoyed it. Whilst smoking he began to think that he would like to know where the rat disappeared to, for he had certain ideas for the morrow not entirely disconnected with a rat-trap. Accordingly, he lit another lamp and placed it so that it would shine well into the right-hand corner of the wall by the fireplace. Then he got all the books he had with him, and placed them handy to throw at the vermin. Finally, he lifted the rope of the alarm bell and placed the end of it on the table, fixing the extreme end under the lamp. As he handled it he could not help noticing how pliable it was, especially for so strong a rope, and one not in use. "You could hang a man with it," he thought to himself. When his preparations were made, he looked around, and said complacently:

"There now, my friend, I think we shall learn something of you this time!" He began his work again, and though as before somewhat disturbed at first by the noise of the rats, soon lost himself in his propositions and problems.

Again he was called to his immediate surroundings suddenly. This time it might not have been the sudden silence only which took his attention; there was a slight movement of the rope, and the lamp moved. Without stirring, he looked to see if his pile of books was within range, and then cast his eye along the rope. As he looked, he saw the great rat drop from the rope on the oak armchair and sit there glaring at him. He raised a book in his right hand, and taking careful aim, flung it at the rat. The latter, with a quick movement, sprang aside and dodged the missile. He then took another book, and a third, and flung them one after another at the rat, but each time unsuccessfully. At last, as he stood with a book poised in his hand to throw, the rat squeaked and seemed afraid. This made Malcolmson more than ever eager to strike, and the book flew and struck the rat a resounding blow. It gave a terrified squeak, and turning on his pursuer a look of terrible malevolence, ran up the chair-back and made a great jump to the rope of the alarm bell and ran up it like lightning. The lamp rocked under the sudden strain, but it was a heavy one and did not topple over. Malcolmson kept his eyes on the rat, and saw it by the light of the second lamp leap to a moulding of the wainscot and disappear through a hole in one of the great pictures which hung on the wall, obscured and invisible through its coating of dirt and dust.

"I shall look up my friend's habitation in the morning," said the student, as he went over to collect his books. "The third picture from the fireplace; I shall not forget." He picked up the books one by one, commenting on them as he lifted them. "*Conic Sections* he does not mind, nor *Cycloidal Oscillations*, nor the *Principia*, nor *Quaternions*, nor *Thermodynamics*. Now for the book that fetched him!" Malcolmson took it up and looked at it. As he did so he started, and a sudden pallor overspread his face. He looked round uneasily and shivered slightly, as he murmured to himself:

"The Bible my mother gave me! What an odd coincidence." He sat down to work again, and the rats in the wainscot renewed their gambols. They did not disturb him, however; somehow their presence gave him a sense of companionship. But he could not attend to his work, and after striving to master the subject on which he was engaged gave it up in despair, and went to bed as the first streak of dawn stole in through the eastern window.

He slept heavily but uneasily, and dreamed much; and when Mrs. Dempster woke him late in the morning, he seemed ill at ease, and for a few minutes did not seem to realize exactly where he was. His first request rather surprised the servant.

"Mrs. Dempster, when I am out to-day I wish you would get the steps and dust or wash those pictures—specially that one the third from the fireplace—I want to see what they are."

Late in the afternoon Malcolmson worked at his books in the shaded walk, and the cheerfulness of the previous day came back to him as the day wore on, and he found that his reading was progressing well. He had worked out to a satisfactory conclusion all the problems which had as yet baffled him, and it was in a state of jubilation that he paid a visit to Mrs. Witham at "The Good Traveller." He found a stranger in the cozy sitting-room with the landlady, who was introduced to him as Dr. Thornhill. She was not quite at ease, and this, combined with the doctor's plunging at once into a series of questions, made Malcolmson come to the conclusion that his presence was not an accident, so without preliminary he said:

"Dr. Thornhill, I shall with pleasure answer you any question you may choose to ask me if you will answer me one question first."

The doctor seemed surprised, but he smiled and answered at once, "Done! What is it?"

"Did Mrs. Witham ask you to come here and see me and advise me?"

Dr. Thornhill for a moment was taken aback, and Mrs. Witham got fiery red and turned away; but the doctor was a frank and ready man, and he answered at once and openly.

"She did: but she didn't intend you to know it. I suppose it was my clumsy haste that made you suspect. She told me that she did not like the idea of your being in that house all by yourself, and that she thought you took too much strong tea. In fact, she wants me to advise you, if possible, to give up the tea and the very late hours. I was a keen student in my time, so I suppose I may take the liberty of a college man, and without offence, advise you not quite as a stranger."

Malcolmson with a bright smile held out his hand. "Shake! as they say in America," he said. "I must thank you for your kindness and Mrs. Witham too, and your kindness deserves a return on my part. I promise to take no more strong tea — no tea at all till you let me — and I shall go to bed tonight at one o'clock at latest. Will that do?"

"Capital," said the doctor. "Now tell us all that you noticed in the old house," and so Malcolmson then and there told in minute detail all that had happened in the last two nights. He was interrupted every now and then by some exclamation from Mrs. Witham, till finally when he told of the episode of the Bible the landlady's pent-up emotions found vent in a shriek; and it was not till a stiff glass of brandy and water had been administered that she grew composed again. Dr. Thornhill listened with a face of growing gravity, and when the narrative was complete and Mrs. Witham had been restored, he asked:

"The rat always went up the rope of the alarm bell?"

"Always."

"I suppose you know," said the Doctor after a pause, "what the rope is?"

"No!"

"It is," said the Doctor slowly, "the very rope which the hangman used for all the victims of the Judge's judicial rancor!" Here he was interrupted by another scream from Mrs. Witham, and steps had to be taken for her recovery. Malcolmson having looked at his watch, and found that it was close to his dinner hour, had gone home before her complete recovery.

When Mrs. Witham was herself again, she almost assailed the Doctor with angry questions as to what he meant by putting such horrible ideas into the poor young man's mind. "He has quite enough there already to upset him," she added. Dr. Thornhill replied:

"My dear madam, I had a distinct purpose in it! I wanted to draw his attention to the bell rope, and to fix it there. It may be that he is in a highly overwrought state, and has been studying too much, although I am bound to say that he seems as sound and healthy a young man, mentally and bodily, as ever I saw — but then the rats — and that suggestion of the devil." The doctor shook his head and went on. "I would have offered to go and stay the first night with him but that I felt sure it would have been a cause of offence. He may get in the night some strange fright or hallucination; and if he does, I want him to pull that rope. All alone as he is it will give us warning, and we may reach him in time to be of service. I shall be sitting up pretty late tonight and shall keep my ears open. Do not be alarmed if Benchurch gets a surprise before morning."

"Oh, Doctor, what do you mean? What do you mean?"

"I mean this; that possibly — nay, more probably — we shall hear the great alarm bell from the Judge's House tonight," and the Doctor made about as effective an exit as could be thought of.

When Malcolmson arrived home he found that it was a little after his usual time, and Mrs. Dempster had gone away — the rules of Greenhow's Charity were not to be neglected. He was glad to see that the place was bright and tidy with a cheerful fire and a

well-trimmed lamp. The evening was colder than might have
been expected in April, and a heavy wind was blowing with such
rapidly-increasing strength that there was every promise of a
storm during the night. For a few minutes after his entrance the
noise of the rats ceased; but so soon as they became accustomed
to his presence they began again. He was glad to hear them, for
he felt once more the feeling of companionship in their noise, and
his mind ran back to the strange fact that they only ceased to
manifest themselves when that other — the great rat with the baleful eyes — came upon the scene. The reading-lamp only was lit
and its green shade kept the ceiling and the upper part of the
room in darkness, so that the cheerful light from the hearth
spreading over the floor and shining on the white cloth laid over
the end of the table was warm and cheery. Malcolmson sat down
to his dinner with a good appetite and a buoyant spirit. After his
dinner and a cigarette, he sat steadily down to work, determined
not to let anything disturb him, for he remembered his promise
to the doctor, and made up his mind to make the best of the time
at his disposal.

For an hour or so he worked all right, and then his thoughts
began to wander from his books. The actual circumstances around
him, the calls on his physical attention, and his nervous susceptibil-
ity were not to be denied. By this time the wind had become a gale,
and the gale a storm. The old house, solid though it was, seemed
to shake to its foundations, and the storm roared and raged through
its many chimneys and its queer old gables, producing strange, un-
earthly sounds in the empty rooms and corridors. Even the great
alarm bell on the roof must have felt the force of the wind, for the
rope rose and fell slightly, as though the bell were moved a little

from time to time and the limber rope fell on the oak floor with a hard and hollow sound.

As Malcolmson listened to it he bethought himself of the doctor's words, "It is the rope which the hangman used for the victims of the Judge's judicial rancor," and he went over to the corner of the fireplace and took it in his hand to look at it. There seemed a sort of deadly interest in it, and as he stood there, he lost himself for a moment in speculation as to who these victims were, and the grim wish of the Judge to have such a ghastly relic ever under his eyes. As he stood there, the swaying of the bell on the roof still lifted the rope now and again; but presently there came a new sensation—a sort of tremor in the rope, as though something was moving along it.

Looking up instinctively Malcolmson saw the great rat coming slowly down towards him, glaring at him steadily. He dropped the rope and started back with a muttered curse, and the rat turning ran up the rope again and disappeared, and at the same instant Malcolmson became conscious that the noise of the rats, which had ceased for a while, began again.

All this set him thinking, and it occurred to him that he had not investigated the lair of the rat or looked at the pictures, as he had intended. He lit the other lamp without the shade, and, holding it up went and stood opposite the third picture from the fireplace on the right-hand side where he had seen the rat disappear on the previous night.

At the first glance he started back so suddenly that he almost dropped the lamp, and a deadly pallor overspread his face. His knees shook, and heavy drops of sweat came on his forehead, and he trembled like an aspen. But he was young and plucky, and pulled himself together, and after the pause of a few seconds stepped forward again, raised the lamp, and examined the picture which had been dusted and washed, and now stood out clearly.

It was of a judge dressed in his robes of scarlet and ermine. His face was strong and merciless, evil, crafty, and vindictive, with a sensual mouth, hooked nose of ruddy color, and shaped like the beak of a bird of prey. The rest of the face was of a cadaverous color. The eyes were of peculiar brilliance and with a terribly malignant expression. As he looked at them, Malcolmson grew cold, for he saw there the very counterpart of the eyes of the great rat. The lamp almost fell from his hand, he saw the rat with its baleful eyes peering out through the hole in the corner of the picture, and noted the sudden cessation of the noise of the other rats. However, he pulled himself together, and went on with his examination of the picture.

The Judge was seated in a great high-backed carved oak chair, on the right-hand side of a great stone fireplace where, in the corner, a rope hung down from the ceiling, its end lying coiled on the floor. With a feeling of something like horror, Malcolmson recognized the scene of the room as it stood, and gazed around him in an awestruck manner as though he expected to find some strange presence behind him. Then he looked over to the corner of the fireplace — and with a loud cry he let the lamp fall from his hand.

There, in the Judge's arm-chair, with the rope hanging behind, sat the rat with the Judge's baleful eyes, now intensified and with a fiendish leer. Save for the howling of the storm without, there was silence.

The fallen lamp recalled Malcolmson to himself. Fortunately, it was of metal, and so the oil was not spilt. However, the practical need of attending to it settled at once his nervous apprehensions.

When he had turned it out, he wiped his brow and thought for a moment.

"This will not do," he said to himself. "If I go on like this, I shall become a crazy fool. This must stop! I promised the doctor I would not take tea. Faith, he was pretty right! My nerves must have been getting into a queer state. Funny I did not notice it. I never felt better in my life. However, it is all right now, and I shall not be such a fool again."

Then he mixed himself a good stiff glass of brandy and water and resolutely sat down to his work.

It was nearly an hour when he looked up from his book, disturbed by the sudden stillness. Without, the wind howled and roared louder than ever, and the rain drove in sheets against the windows, beating like hail on the glass; but within there was no sound whatever save the echo of the wind as it roared in the great chimney, and now and then a hiss as a few raindrops found their way down the chimney in a lull of the storm. The fire had fallen low and had ceased to flame, though it threw out a red glow. Malcolmson listened attentively, and presently heard a thin, squeaking noise, very faint. It came from the corner of the room where the rope hung down, and he thought it was the creaking of the rope on the floor as the swaying of the bell raised and lowered it. Looking up, however, he saw in the dim light the great rat clinging to the rope and gnawing it. The rope was already nearly gnawed through — he could see the lighter color where the strands were laid bare. As he looked the job was completed, and the severed end of the rope fell clattering on the oaken floor, whilst for an instant the great rat remained like a knob or tassel at the end of the rope, which now began to sway to and fro. Malcolmson felt for a

moment another pang of terror as he thought that now the possibility of calling the outer world to his assistance was cut off, but an intense anger took its place, and seizing the book he was reading he hurled it at the rat. The blow was well aimed, but before the missile could reach him the rat dropped off and struck the floor with a soft thud. Malcolmson instantly rushed over towards him, but it darted away and disappeared in the darkness of the shadows of the room. Malcolmson felt that his work was over for the night, and determined then and there to vary the monotony of the proceedings by a hunt for the rat, and took off the green shade of the lamp so as to insure a wider spreading light. As he did so the gloom of the upper part of the room was relieved, and in the new flood of light, great by comparison with the previous darkness, the pictures on the wall stood out boldly. From where he stood, Malcolmson saw right opposite to him the third picture on the wall from the right of the fireplace. He rubbed his eyes in surprise, and then a great fear began to come upon him.

In the center of the picture was a great irregular patch of brown canvas, as fresh as when it was stretched on the frame. The background was as before, with chair and chimney-corner and rope, but the figure of the Judge had disappeared.

Malcolmson, almost in a chill of horror, turned slowly round, and then he began to shake and tremble like a man in a palsy. His strength seemed to have left him, and he was incapable of action or movement, hardly even of thought. He could only see and hear.

There, on the great high-backed carved oak chair sat the Judge in his robes of scarlet and ermine, with his baleful eyes glaring vindictively, and a smile of triumph on the resolute, cruel mouth, as he lifted with his hands a *black cap*. Malcolmson felt as if the blood was running from his heart, as one does in moments of prolonged suspense. There was a singing in his ears. Without, he could hear the roar and howl of the tempest, and through it, swept on the storm, came the striking of midnight by the great chimes in the market place. He stood for a space of time that seemed to him endless still as a statue, and with wide-open, horror-struck eyes, breathless. As the clock struck, so the smile of triumph on the Judge's face intensified, and at the last stroke of midnight he placed the black cap on his head.

Slowly and deliberately the Judge rose from his chair and picked up the piece of the rope of the alarm bell which lay on the floor, drew it through his hands as if he enjoyed its touch, and then deliberately began to knot one end of it, fashioning it into a noose. This he tightened and tested with his foot, pulling hard at it till he was satisfied and then making a running noose of it, which he held in his hand. Then he began to move along the table on the opposite side to Malcolmson keeping his eyes on him until he had passed him, when with a quick movement he stood in front of the door. Malcolmson then began to feel that he was trapped, and tried to think of what he should do. There was some fascination in the Judge's eyes, which he never took off him, and he had, perforce, to look. He saw the Judge approach—still keeping between him and the door—and raise the noose and throw it towards him as if to entangle him. With a great effort he made a quick movement to one side, and saw the rope fall beside him, and heard it strike the oaken floor. Again the Judge raised the noose and tried to ensnare him, ever keeping his baleful eyes fixed on him, and each time by a mighty effort the student just managed to evade it. So this went on for many times, the Judge seeming

never discouraged nor discomposed at failure, but playing as a cat does with a mouse. At last in despair, which had reached its climax, Malcolmson cast a quick glance round him. The lamp seemed to have blazed up, and there was a fairly good light in the room. At the many rat-holes and in the chinks and crannies of the wainscot he saw the rats' eyes; and this aspect, that was purely physical, gave him a gleam of comfort. He looked around and saw that the rope of the great alarm bell was laden with rats. Every inch of it was covered with them, and more and more were pouring through the small circular hole in the ceiling whence it emerged, so that with their weight the bell was beginning to sway.

Hark! it had swayed till the clapper had touched the bell. The sound was but a tiny one, but the bell was only beginning to sway, and it would increase.

At the sound the Judge, who had been keeping his eyes fixed on Malcolmson, looked up, and a scowl of diabolical anger overspread his face. His eyes fairly glowed like hot coals, and he stamped his foot with a sound that seemed to make the house shake. A dreadful peal of thunder broke overhead as he raised the rope again, whilst the rats kept running up and down the rope as though working against time. This time, instead of throwing it, he drew close to his victim, and held open the noose as he approached. As he came closer there seemed something paralyzing in his very presence, and Malcolmson stood rigid as a corpse. He felt the Judge's icy fingers touch his throat as he adjusted the rope. The noose tightened — tightened. Then the Judge, taking the rigid form of the student in his arms, carried him over and placed him standing in the oak chair, and stepping up beside him, put his hand up and caught the end of the swaying rope of the alarm bell. As he

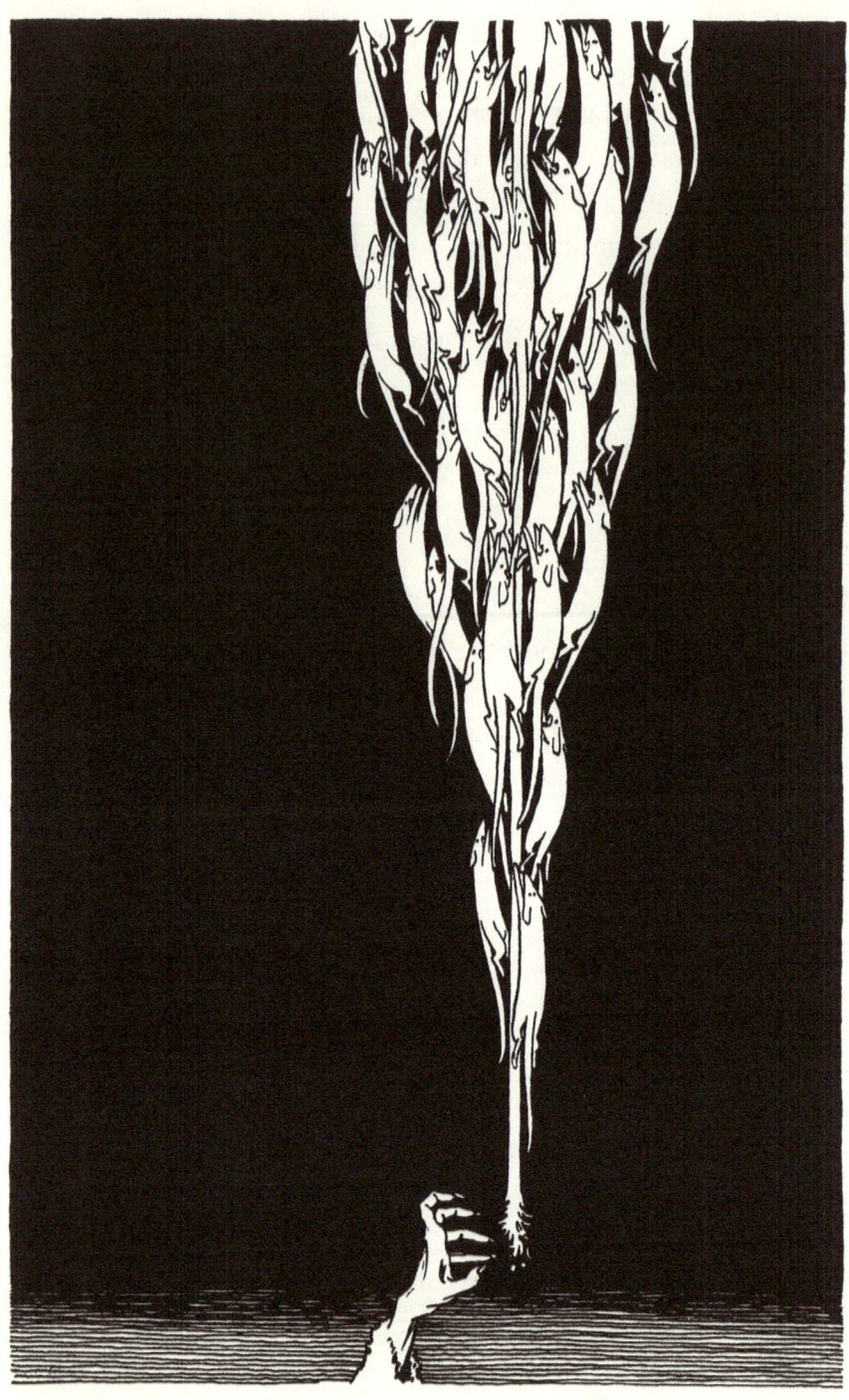

raised his hand the rats fled squeaking, and disappeared through the hole in the ceiling. Taking the end of the noose which was round Malcolmson's neck he tied it to the hanging-bell rope, and then, descending, pulled away the chair.

When the alarm bell of the Judge's House began to sound, a crowd soon assembled. Lights and torches of various kinds appeared, and soon a silent crowd was hurrying to the spot. They knocked loudly at the door, but there was no reply. Then they burst in the door, and poured into the great dining-room, the doctor at the head.

There at the end of the rope of the great alarm bell hung the body of the student, and on the face of the Judge in the picture was a malignant smile.

GIBBET HILL

WHEN I LEFT the Royal Huts Inn, on the top of Hind Head, in order to visit the Devil's Punchbowl and Gibbet Hill, immortalized by Turner in the *Liber Studiorium*, I passed along a wide straight road — the new high road between London and Portsmouth — and shortly came to the edge of the Punchbowl and feasted my eyes on its beauty. The fog, which had been heavy in London when I left on this mid-October morning, extended even to Haslemere and hung in the valleys so that the tops of the Surrey hills rose like islands from the sea of mist, and in the brilliant sunshine which glorified these upper levels softened and mellowed all the wide expanse of hill and dale and down, which ranged between me and the Southern coast. The hill gave steeply on all sides save the north-west, where the circular valley opened to the plain below.

All the summer tints were chastened and mellowed; all the full colors which the sunshine had glorified had faded into the sere of Autumn. The pink and purple of the heather were changed to a brown with only a suggestion of faded color to warm its tone. The bracken was of rich amber and faded yellow, and the myriads of grasses and wild flowers had donned their winter garb—the hues of decay. Through all this rich mass of Autumn tints, the broom, untouched as yet by the frost, sent an emerald flash. The green bushes which fringed the tiny stream running through the valley seemed of supernatural vividness, and the dark green of the pines which covered the western slope and ran down into the valley seemed to assert in some positive way the right of nature to maintain her own color despite all influences. Away to the north and west, past the spurs and shoulders of the hill, the woods and valleys, the copses and villages and hills and ridges ranged in endless succession; and it was after a long, long pause that I turned from drinking in the beauty of the scene with my heart full of the power and majesty and purifying influence of nature's beauty. "Here at least," said I to myself, "the soul of man is elevated; and on this higher plane of nature's handiwork the evil of our hearts is lulled."

As I turned, however, I started, for, as if by the irony of fate, there, beside me, was a grim memorial of man's wickedness and lust for blood—a tombstone by the roadside, marking the spot where a century ago a poor seaman trudging on his way from Portsmouth was murdered.

But not the stone only was of interest; for by it were three figures which would have arrested attention anywhere. They were only children, but of types that were not common. Two were young Indian girls of an age which by the slower development of English girlhood would be about some thirteen or fourteen years; being, however, of Eastern birth, they were probably much younger. They stood one on each side of the memorial stone, looking almost like heraldic supporters, as each with a slim brown hand resting on an elbow of the stone, leaned her face on the hand while looking at me gravely with long, dark, fathomless eyes. They were both very pretty of their type, and their slim girlish figures were draped in black of some shimmering material, made in a half Eastern fashion with a wide belt of the stuff round the waist, and some kind of dark material wound around the head and acting as a head gear. The third of the group was a little boy of some ten years old, with hair of spun gold, eyes like blue porcelain, and a winning smile on his rosy face. One might designate him indifferently a Cupid or an angel. He was dressed in a dark blood-colored tunic.

For a few seconds I stood looking at this group, they regarding me steadfastly without the slightest movement. Then I spoke to them, making some remark about the beauty of the scene. One of the girls said, tapping the stone with her hand as she spoke.

"Can you tell us anything about this stone, Sir? We are strangers."

"I am a stranger here myself, but I think we will find it here," I answered, as I proceeded to read the inscription, which is on both sides of the stone. When I read of the word murder they all three looked at each other and then at me, and shuddered, and, strange to say, followed the shudder with a smile, I thought they might be frightened, and I hastened to add—"But you need not let this disturb you. It all happened a hundred years ago, when the country was very different from what it is now." One of the girls said in a low voice, whose tones were peculiarly penetrating:

"I hope not—I trust not;" and the little boy looked up at me with a laugh and said:

"I suppose if there were a murder now, some one would be stuck up on Gibbet Hill!"

"Hullo! young man," said I, "You know all about it, I see. I am going up to the hill top to see the Memorial Cross. Will you come and see where they put the murderer?"

"With pleasure," he said, with an air of almost supernatural gravity, lifting his cap in acknowledgment of my invitation. The girls bowed too, and we all moved up the hill together. As we went, I noticed that the boy had one of his hands tightly clenched. "What have you got there?" I asked of him.

"These!" he said, opening his hand and showing me a crumpled mass of great earthworms, wriggling in their sudden freedom. "I love worms," he went on. "See! they wriggle so, and you can pull them out long!" and he illustrated the latter fact.

"Poor worms!" said I, "Why not let them go? They would much rather be on the ground."

"Shan't," was his only reply, as he shoved them into the folds of his tunic.

There were a lot of persons at the cross when we reached the top of Gibbet Hill, besides abundant evidence of recent visitors in the shape of egg-shells and pieces of newspaper—for the cross is a favorite picnicking spot. Amongst the strangers my fancy was chiefly taken by a lady and gentleman whom I dubbed "the honeymoon couple." I soon became so absorbed by the lovely view which lay stretched before me—a wilderness of rising hill-tops with green woods and rich valleys—that I quite forgot my young companions. I went to the edge of the steep hill and sat down looking eastwards, and lost myself in the beauty of the scene.

Presently I remembered my young companions, and looked around for them; but they had quite disappeared: there was not a sight of them anywhere around.

My departure from London had been early, and the walk from Haslemere in the blazing October sun a little fatiguing, so, after a while, when I had been all around the summit of the Head and had, so to speak, boxed the scenic compass, I took my way to a deep shady grove of hazel and beech with tall pines rising over all — one of those dense copses that creep up from the valley, throwing jagged spikes of greenery up the slopes of the hill. Here there was the very perfection of autumn fullness. The undergrowth grew luxuriantly under the shelter of the clustering pines. The brown of the bark and the bluish bloom of the foliage of the pines, as one gazed into the half dim aisles between them — the sweet aromatic odor which they exhaled — the sleepy silence accentuated only by the hum of nature's myriad vitalities — the soft, rich grass, whose summer greenery stood untouched as yet in this sheltered dell — all invited to repose. With a blissful feeling of content, I stretched myself on the grass, and soon lost my thoughts and my consciousness in the interlaced branches above me.

How long I slept I know not; but it must have been a good while, for I felt thoroughly refreshed as to brain and with that half-aching sense of cramped muscles which comes after a long period of unchanged attitude; and there was over me that mysterious sense of elapsed time which tells philosophers that our thought is continuous in some form or another. There was, however, no sense of duty omitted — no press of coming work, which in such cases destroys the charm of awaking. I knew that there was ample time before me, and that I might muse on, unchecked, that I could revel to my heart's content in the sense of freedom, and enjoy the freshness and purity of the air in this wonderful spot.

And so, I did not stir, but lay on my back with my hands under my head looking up into the branches and watching the gleams of light struggle through the tracery of leaf and branch. I thought of many things, in that luxurious half-dreamy way which belongs to the leisure of an habitually busy man. Taking up a thread of thought and dropping it again — swaying between general and particular ideas — in all ways realizing that greatest of pleasures, intellectual *laissez aller.*

There was in the air the same faint hum of varied sounds which had at the first lulled me to sleep; but somehow the volume was richer than before — more full and satisfying to the ear, and with a special significance, as if not only all nature was speaking but that there was some one voice amongst the myriad more potent than the rest. I listened with a growing interest, and the sound seemed to take a more definite place amongst nature's harmonies. It was not as if it grew in loudness, but merely as if the vibrations accumulated, coming in waves more quickly than they could die away.

Gradually all the other noises seemed to die away, and I heard only this one sound. It seemed to be closer and closer as I began to distinguish more clearly, until I shortly came to the conclusion that its source was separated from me by only some score of yards. Then I began to be able to analyze it a little. In general effect it was like a sort of musical muffled corncrake — a corncrake in a whisper — but with some subtle prevailing sweetness which seemed of almost irresistible attraction. Presently I raised my head from amongst the bracken where I lay, and looked whence the sound proceeded.

There, to my surprise, in an open dell where the light fell through a break in the trees were grouped the children whom I had seen. The two girls were seated, and between them the little boy stood up. One of the girls held in her left hand something which looked like a set of pandean pipes made of thin canes but slightly thicker than wheaten straws. Across this she drew something attached to the fingers of the right hand, which made the bass of the strange corncrake sound. The other girl held a shell with strings across it which she touched lightly; and the boy had a sort of reed flute which gave forth a peculiarly long sweet note, but which blended in the mass of music. Then the girls joined in a sort of monotonous chant of strange sweetness but very, very faint. They were all three looking well to one side of me. By and by the girls stood up; they all turned slightly, and I could see that they were evidently turning slowly in a complete circle, as though seeking in every direction around them. As they began to face my direction, I sank down again into the bracken so that they might not see me, for the affair began to absorb my interest. I took care, however, to peep through the fronds of the bracken and see all that went on. A very short time elapsed before my attention was diverted, and in not the most pleasant of ways.

Hearing a stir and rustle among the dead leaves beside me I looked round, and almost jumped to my feet, for there close by, and approaching closer, was a large snake of the blindworm species. It came straight towards me and actually passed over my feet. I did not stir, and it went on, heeding me no more than if I had been a log of wood, and wriggled away towards the group in the sunlit glade. It was evidently attracted by the strange, weird music, and as this was my first actual experience of serpent-charming, my interest grew, and I watched the little party more closely than before. They went on with their music, and the snake approached closer and closer; till at the feet of the fair-haired child it stopped, and, curling itself into a spiral, raised its head and began to hiss. The boy looked down, and the girls turned their eyes towards him, but the music did not stop for a moment; on the contrary, it grew something quicker. Then the snake twined itself around the child's ankle and began to climb its way up his body, wriggling round and round his leg and thigh, and up and up, till at last it crawled along the arm that held the flute.

Then, suddenly, the music stopped. The two girls stood up, and the boy stretched out his arm with the snake wound around it, with his hand stretched out wide open, the palm upwards. The snake remained perfectly still, as if transformed into stone. Then the girls took hands and circled slowly around the boy, uttering a low, whispering, mysterious chant, something the same as the earlier one, but this time in decrescendo as compared with the former crescendo, and in a minor key. This went on for quite two or three minutes. The boy remained perfectly still, with his arm extended, and his blue eyes fixed on the snake. Then the latter raised its head slightly and seemed to follow with it the movements of the circling girls. They continued their slow movement, round and round, the snake's movements being more and more pronounced with each revolution, till presently it was boldly turning, like the automatic motion of a firework, around the boy's arm. Gradually the motion of the girls got slower and that of the snake correspondingly less, till, presently, the girls' movement, and the low crooning music, which had never stopped, died away altogether, and the snake hung, a dead mass as limp as a piece of string, across the boy's

hand. The boy never moved, but the girls let go each other's hands, and one of them, who had stopped just in front of the boy, took the snake by head and tail and seemed to gently pull it out straight. When she let it go, it lay across the boy's hand as stiff as a piece of wood. There was something uncanny about this which recalled to me recollections of a man whom I had once seen in a cataleptic fit, and whose body retained any position into which it was put, no matter how grotesque or how uncomfortable or strained. The snake seemed to be under some similar condition, and with strange curiosity I awaited the next development. The boy continued impassive, his hand still stretched out and the snake resting across it. The girls stood a little in front of and on either side of him, so that the outstretched hand was midway between them.

Then began some questioning between them in a language which I presumed to be some form of Indian, but which I did not understand. Both voices were sweet, with a peculiar penetrating power, but one of them I seemed instinctively to fear, although it was the sweeter and softer of the two. Somehow — and the idea was quite spontaneous — it seemed to suggest murder. From the tones and inflections of the voices, I gathered that all utterances were put in the form of questions — a supposition shortly confirmed in a strange way, for the answers were given by the rigid snake. When each girl in turn had had her say — and they suggested positive and negative in their tones — the snake would slowly turn around like the needle in a compass, and point its head to either one. The sweeter voice seemed to be the positive, and the other the negative in the inquiry; and in all the earlier questions the snake, after turning slowly around, remained with its head towards the negative. This first seemed to disturb and then annoy the positive inquirer, and her voice grew more deadly sweet and penetrating until it made me shudder. Then she seemed to get more and more enraged, for her eyes gleamed with a dark unholy light, and at the last came her question in a keen thrilling whisper. For answer the snake then spun round quicker and quicker, and suddenly came to a dead stop in front of the other girl.

The disappointed one gave one fierce, short, sharp sound like a dog's bark, whilst a look of deadly malice swept over her face; and then passed away, leaving it as serene as before. At the same instant the rigidity of the snake collapsed, and it hung for an instant as limp as before, and then slipped to the ground, and lay there all in a heap without motion, as if dead. The boy started, as though from sleep to waking, and began to laugh. The girls joined in the cachinnation, and in an instant the glade, which had seemed so weird, grew instinct with laughter, as the children chased each other into the recesses of the wood and disappeared from view.

Then I rose up from the bracken where I lay. I could hardly believe my eyes, and thought that I must have been sleeping, and have dreamt it all. But there lay the seemingly dead snake before me as a palpable evidence that I had beheld a reality.

The sun was far in the west when I had finished my stroll through the laneways and copses upon the Witley side of Hind Head and found myself once more at its highest point on Gibbet Hill.

The place was now deserted. The picnickers had all gone home; the pony traps and donkeys and parties of school children had disappeared, and nothing remained of the day's visitation but the usual increase in old newspapers and broken egg shells. As the light was just beginning to fade and the air to grow a shade colder, the sense of loneliness was more than ever marked. But I had come from the midst of the hum and turmoil of the city to enjoy this very loneliness, and its luxury was to me unspeakable. Down in the valleys the mist still lay dim and fleecy white, and from it the hill tops rose dark and grim. A belt of cloud fringed the whole horizon, and above it stretched a sea of sulfur yellow, flecked here and there with little clouds of white which, swimming high above the level of the hill, caught the last splendors of the sun, now obscured by the horizon. One or two stars began to twinkle through the darkening sky, and a stillness that seemed sentient stole up through the valley and reached to where I sat.

Then the air grew colder, and the silence became perfect. The stars swam out into the sky, which had now a darker blue, and a soft light fell on the scene. I sat on and on, and drank in the wondrous beauty in which I was immersed. Weariness of mind and body seemed of the dim past and as if they could never again be other than a sad memory. In such moments a man seems almost to be born again, and to have every faculty renewed to the full. I leaned with my back against the great stone cross, and, putting my hands behind me, clasped my arms around its back so as to change my position and be able to enjoy more fully the luxury of rest.

Suddenly, without a word of warning, each hand was grasped from behind and held tight in a pair of hands, thin and warm but so strong that I could make no movement; and at the same time a scarf or shawl of some light, fleecy, but thick material was thrown over my face and drawn tightly from behind, holding my head close to the stone. So pinioned and gagged, I could neither move nor speak, and had perforce to await the coming events. Then my hands were tied with a string put around the wrists and drawn tight, so that I was fixed more firmly than before. I could hear no sound, and took it for granted that I was being prepared for robbery. I was alone, far away from everyone and in the hands of men stronger than I was myself, and so resigned myself to the situation as well as I could — secretly thankful that I had only a small sum of money with me. After a time which seemed long, but which was probably of but a few minutes' duration, the scarf was pulled down so far that my eyes were free, though my mouth was still covered and I was unable to cry out.

For a few moments I was too much surprised even to think as strange what I saw before me. Instead of burly footpads with rude manner and coarse force, there were the three children who had arrested my attention earlier in the day. They stood before me perfectly still and silent for a little while, their eyes being the only features which expressed either consciousness or interest of any kind. Two of them, the boy and one girl, then smiled on me with an amused superiority, whilst the other — she who in the glade had exhibited such anger — smiled with a deadly cold hate which, bound as I was, made me shudder. This latter then approached me closer, the others remaining quite still and looking on with their superior amused smile. She took from her waist, where it was concealed in the folds of her dress, a long sharp dagger, thin, double-edged, and lethal-looking. This she proceeded to flourish before me with extraordinary dexterity and rapidity. Half the time its keen edge actually touched my skin, and the contact made me wince. Anon she would dart towards my eyes till I could feel its cold point actually touching my eyeballs. Then she would as if hurl herself at me with the point of the deadly weapon directed to my heart, but would stop just as it seemed that my last moment had

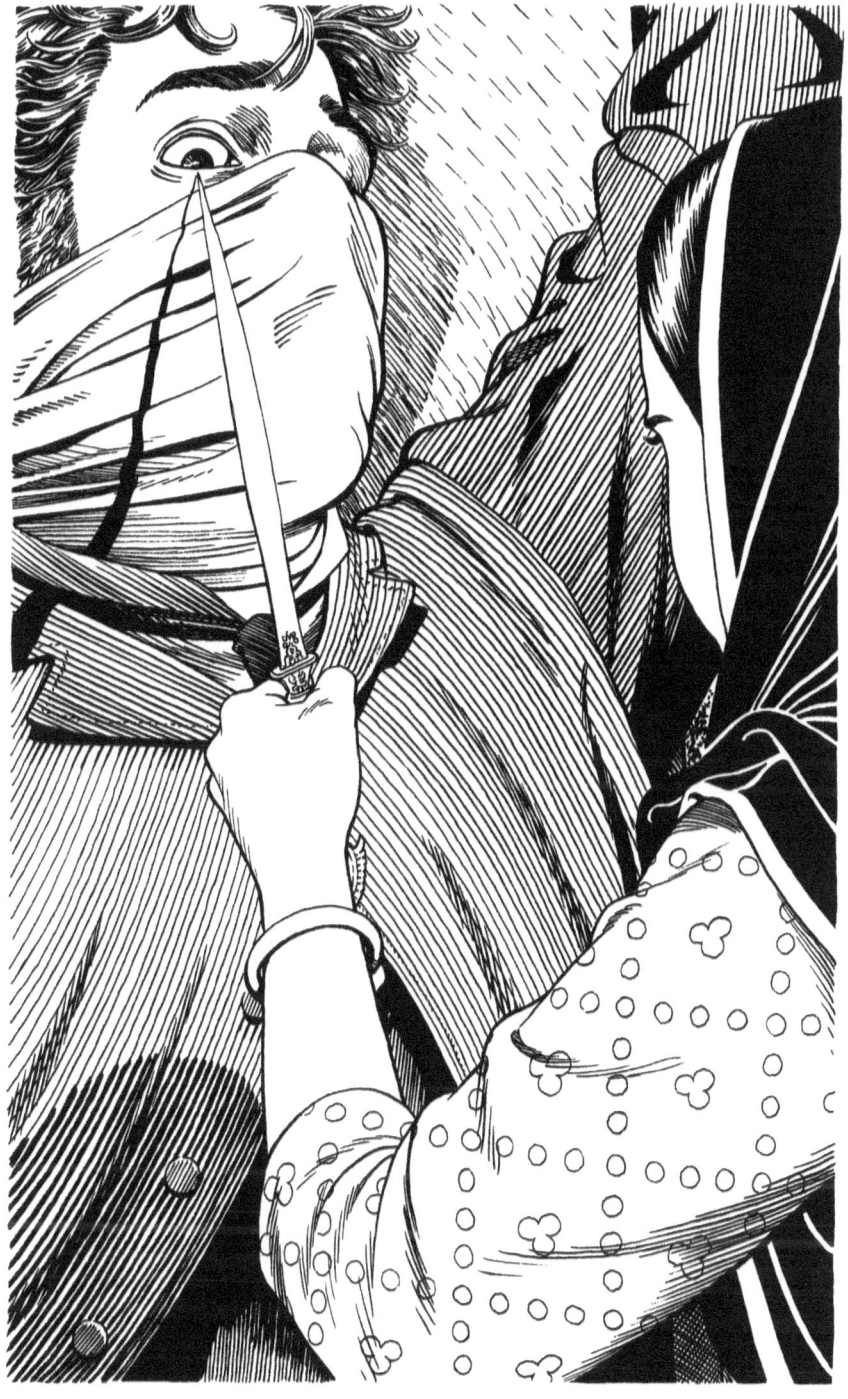

come. This went on for a little while; but short though it was, it seemed endless. I felt a cold chill, a strange numbness, growing over me; my heart seemed to get cold and weak — colder, and colder — weaker and weaker, still, till at length my eyes closed. I tried to open them — succeeded; tried again — failed, succeeded — failed — and at length consciousness passed away from me.

The last thing I remember seeing with my waking eyes was the gleam of the long knife in the starlight as it moved in the young girl's dexterous play. The last sound I heard was a low laugh from all three of the children.

The voice in my ears was dim and distant; but it gradually grew louder, and the spoken words became intelligible: —

"Wake up! — Wake up, man! You will get your death of cold!"

Cold! The word struck home, for there was at my heart a numbness, and a chill as of death. My consciousness struggled back into existence, and I opened my eyes.

It was now much brighter, for a great yellow moon had arisen, and the common was flooded with its light. Beside me were two persons whom at once I recognized as "the honeymoon couple" of earlier in the day. The man was bending over me, and was shaking me roughly by the shoulder, whilst the lady stood by, looking on anxiously, with her hands clasped.

"He is not dead, George, is he?" I heard her say. The answer came.

"No! thank goodness! — he must have fallen asleep. It is a mercy that you had the inspiration to come out to see the moonlight view from here; he might have died of cold. See! the ground is white with the hoar-frost already. Wake up, man! — Wake up, and come away!"

"My heart," I murmured, "My heart!" for it was icy cold. The man looked more serious, and said to his wife: —

"Bella, this may be serious. Could you run back to the hotel, and send some one if necessary? It may be that his heart is affected."

"Certainly, dear; shall I go at once?"

"Wait a minute first." He leant over me again. The past was coming back to me quickly, and I asked him:

"Did you see anywhere some children, two Indian girls, and a fair-haired boy?"

"Yes! hours and hours ago, as they went down the London road on a tricycle. They were laughing, and we thought them the prettiest and happiest children we had ever seen. But why?"

"My heart! my heart!" I cried out again, for there was a coldness, which seemed to numb me.

The man put his hand over my heart, but quickly tore it away again with a cry of terror.

"What is it, George? what is it?" almost shrieked the lady, for his action was so sudden and unexpected, that it thoroughly frightened her.

He stood back, and she clung frightened to his arm, as a large blindworm wriggled itself out from my bosom—fell on the ground—and glided away down the hillside into the copse below.

THE SQUAW

NURNBERG AT THE TIME was not so much exploited as it has been since then. Irving had not been playing *Faust,* and the very name of the old town was hardly known to the great bulk of the travelling public. My wife and I being in the second week of our honeymoon, naturally wanted someone else to join our party, so that when the cheery stranger, Elias P. Hutcheson, hailing from Isthmian City, Bleeding Gulch, Maple Tree County, Neb., turned up at the station at Frankfort, and casually remarked that he was going on to see the most all-fired old Methuselah of a town in Yur-rup, and that he guessed that so much traveling alone was enough to send an intelligent, active citizen into the melancholy ward of a daft house, we took the pretty broad hint and suggested that we should join forces. We found, on comparing notes afterwards, that we had each intended to speak with some diffidence or hesitation so as not to appear too eager, such not being a good compliment to the success of our married life; but the effect was entirely marred by our both beginning to speak at the same instant—stopping simultaneously and then going on together again. Anyhow, no matter how, it was done; and Elias P. Hutcheson became one of our party. Straightway Amelia and I found the pleasant benefit; instead of quarrelling, as we had been doing, we found that the restraining influence of a third party was such that we now took every opportunity of spooning in odd corners. Amelia declares that ever since she has, as the result of that experience, advised all her friends to take a friend on the honeymoon. Well, we "did" Nurnberg together, and much enjoyed the racy remarks of our transatlantic friend, who, from his quaint speech and his wonderful stock of adventures, might have stepped out of a novel. We kept for the last object of interest in the city to be visited the Burg, and on the day appointed for the visit strolled round the outer wall of the city by the eastern side.

The Burg is seated on a rock dominating the town and an immensely deep fosse guards it on the northern side. Nurnberg has been happy in that it was never sacked; had it been it would certainly not be so spick and span perfect as it is at present. The ditch has not been used for centuries, and now its base is spread with tea-gardens and orchards, of which some of the trees are of quite respectable growth. As we wandered round the wall, dawdling in the hot July sunshine, we often paused to admire the views spread before us, and in especial the great plain covered with towns and villages and bounded with a blue line of hills, like a landscape of Claude Lorraine. From this we always turned with new delight to the city itself, with its myriad of quaint old gables and acre-wide red roofs dotted with dormer windows, tier upon tier. A little to our right rose the towers of the Burg, and nearer still, standing grim, the Torture Tower, which was, and is, perhaps, the most interesting place in the city. For centuries the tradition of the Iron Virgin of Nurnberg has been handed down as an instance of the horrors of cruelty of which man is capable; we had long looked forward to seeing it; and here at last was its home.

In one of our pauses, we leaned over the wall of the moat and looked down. The garden seemed quite fifty or sixty feet below us, and the sun pouring into it with an intense, moveless heat like that of an oven. Beyond rose the grey, grim wall seemingly of endless height, and losing itself right and left in the angles of bastion and counterscarp. Trees and bushes crowned the wall, and above again towered the lofty houses on whose massive beauty Time has only set the hand of approval. The sun was hot and we were lazy; time was our own, and we lingered, leaning on the wall. Just below us was a pretty sight—a great black cat lying stretched in the sun, whilst round her gamboled prettily a tiny black kitten. The mother would wave her tail for the kitten to play with, or would raise her feet and push away the little one as an encouragement to further play. They were just at the foot of the wall, and Elias P. Hutcheson, in order to help the play, stooped and took from the walk a moderate sized pebble.

"See!" he said, "I will drop it near the kitten, and they will both wonder where it came from."

"Oh, be careful," said my wife; "you might hit the dear little thing!"

"Not me, ma'am," said Elias P. "Why, I'm as tender as a Maine cherry-tree. Lor, bless ye. I wouldn't hurt the poor pooty little critter

more'n I'd scalp a baby. An' you may bet your variegated socks on that! See, I'll drop it fur away on the outside so's not to go near her!" Thus saying, he leaned over and held his arm out at full length and dropped the stone. It may be that there is some attractive force which draws lesser matters to greater; or more probably that the wall was not plump but sloped to its base — we not noticing the inclination from above; but the stone fell with a sickening thud that came up to us through the hot air, right on the kitten's head, and shattered out its little brains then and there. The black cat cast a swift upward glance, and we saw her eyes like green fire fixed an instant on Elias P. Hutcheson; and then her attention was given to the kitten, which lay still with just a quiver of her tiny limbs, whilst a thin red stream trickled from a gaping wound. With a muffled cry, such as a human being might give, she bent over the kitten, licking its wounds and moaning. Suddenly she seemed to realize that it was dead, and again threw her eyes up at us. I shall never forget the sight, for she looked the perfect incarnation of hate. Her green eyes blazed with lurid fire, and the white, sharp teeth seemed to almost shine through the blood which dabbled her mouth and whiskers. She gnashed her teeth, and her claws stood out stark and at full length on every paw. Then she made a wild rush up the wall as if to reach us, but when the momentum ended, fell back and further added to her horrible appearance, for she fell on the kitten and rose with her black fur smeared with its brains and blood. Amelia turned quite faint, and I had to lift her back from the wall. There was a seat close by in shade of a spreading plane-tree, and here I placed her whilst she composed herself. Then I went back to Hutcheson, who stood without moving, looking down on the angry cat below.

As I joined him, he said:

"Wall, I guess that air the savagest beast I ever see—'cept once when an Apache squaw had an edge on a half-breed what they nicknamed 'Splinters' 'cos of the way he fixed up her papoose which he stole on a raid just to show that he appreciated the way they had given his mother the fire torture. She got that kinder look so set on her face that it jest seemed to grow there. She followed Splinters mor'n three year till at last the braves got him and handed him over to her. They did say that no man, white or Injun, had ever been so long a-dying under the tortures of the Apaches. The only time I ever see her smile was when I wiped her out. I kem on the camp just in time to see Splinters pass in his checks, and he wasn't sorry to go either. He was a hard citizen, and though I never could shake with him after that papoose business—for it was bitter bad, and he should have been a white man, for he looked like one—I see he had got paid out in full. Durn me, but I took a piece of his hide from one of his skinnin' posts an' had it made into a pocket-book. It's here now!" and he slapped the breast pocket of his coat.

Whilst he was speaking the cat was continuing her frantic efforts to get up the wall. She would take a run back and then charge up, sometimes reaching an incredible height. She did not seem to mind the heavy fall which she got each time but started with renewed vigor; and at every tumble her appearance became more horrible. Hutcheson was a kind-hearted man—my wife and I had both noticed little acts of kindness to animals as well as to persons—and he seemed concerned at the state of fury to which the cat had wrought herself.

"Wall, now!" he said, "I du declare that that poor critter seems quite desperate. There! there! poor thing, it was all an accident—

though that won't bring back your little one to you. Say! I wouldn't have had such a thing happen for a thousand! Just shows what a clumsy fool of a man can do when he tries to play! Seems I'm too darned slipperhanded to even play with a cat. Say, Colonel!" it was a pleasant way he had to bestow titles freely—"I hope your wife don't hold no grudge against me on account of this unpleasantness? Why, I wouldn't have had it occur on no account."

He came over to Amelia and apologized profusely, and she with her usual kindness of heart hastened to assure him that she quite understood that it was an accident. Then we all went again to the wall and looked over.

The cat, missing Hutcheson's face, had drawn back across the moat, and was sitting on her haunches as though ready to spring. Indeed, the very instant she saw him she did spring, and with a blind unreasoning fury, which would have been grotesque, only that it was so frightfully real. She did not try to run up the wall, but simply launched herself at him as though hate and fury could lend her wings to pass straight through the great distance between them. Amelia, womanlike, got quite concerned, and said to Elias P. in a warning voice:

"Oh! you must be very careful. That animal would try to kill you if she were here; her eyes look like positive murder."

He laughed out jovially. "Excuse me, ma'am," he said, "but I can't help laughin'. Fancy a man that has fought grizzlies an' Injuns bein' careful of bein' murdered by a cat!"

When the cat heard him laugh, her whole demeanor seemed to change. She no longer tried to jump or run up the wall, but went quietly over, and sitting again beside the dead kitten began to lick and fondle it as though it were alive.

"See!" said I, "the effect of a really strong man. Even that animal in the midst of her fury recognizes the voice of a master, and bows to him!"

"Like a squaw!" was the only comment of Elias P. Hutcheson, as we moved on our way round the city fosse. Every now and then we looked over the wall and each time saw the cat following us. At first, she had kept going back to the dead kitten, and then as the distance grew greater took it in her mouth and so followed. After a while, however, she abandoned this, for we saw her following all alone; she had evidently hidden the body somewhere. Amelia's alarm grew at the cat's persistence, and more than once she repeated her warning; but the American always laughed with amusement, till finally, seeing that she was beginning to be worried, he said:

"I say, ma'am, you needn't be skeered over that cat. I go heeled, I du!" Here he slapped his pistol pocket at the back of his lumbar region. "Why sooner'n have you worried, I'll shoot the critter, right here, an' risk the police interferin' with a citizen of the United States for carryin' arms contrairy to reg'lations!" As he spoke, he looked over the wall, but the cat on seeing him, retreated, with a growl, into a bed of tall flowers, and was hidden. He went on: "Blest if that 'ar critter ain't got more sense of what's good for her than most Christians. I guess we've seen the last of her! You bet, she'll go back now to that busted kitten and have a private funeral of it, all to herself!"

Amelia did not like to say more, lest he might, in mistaken kindness to her, fulfil his threat of shooting the cat: and so we went on and crossed the little wooden bridge leading to the gateway whence ran the steep paved roadway between the Burg and the pentagonal Torture Tower. As we crossed the bridge we saw the cat again down below us. When she saw us, her fury seemed to return, and

she made frantic efforts to get up the steep wall. Hutcheson laughed
as he looked down at her, and said:

"Goodbye, old girl. Sorry I injured your feelin's, but you'll get
over it in time! So long!" And then we passed through the long, dim
archway and came to the gate of the Burg.

When we came out again after our survey of this most beautiful
old place which not even the well-intentioned efforts of the Gothic
restorers of forty years ago have been able to spoil—though their
restoration was then glaring white—we seemed to have quite forgotten the unpleasant episode of the morning. The old lime tree
with its great trunk gnarled with the passing of nearly nine centuries, the deep well cut through the heart of the rock by those cap-
tives of old, and the lovely view from the city wall whence we
heard, spread over almost a full quarter of an hour, the multitudi-
nous chimes of the city, had all helped to wipe out from our minds
the incident of the slain kitten.

We were the only visitors who had entered the Torture Tower
that morning—so at least said the old custodian—and as we had
the place all to ourselves were able to make a minute and more satisfactory survey than would have otherwise been possible. The custodian, looking to us as the sole source of his gains for the day, was
willing to meet our wishes in any way. The Torture Tower is truly
a grim place, even now when many thousands of visitors have sent
a stream of life, and the joy that follows life, into the place; but at
the time I mention it wore its grimmest and most gruesome aspect.
The dust of ages seemed to have settled on it, and the darkness and
the horror of its memories seem to have become sentient in a way
that would have satisfied the Pantheistic souls of Philo or Spinoza.
The lower chamber where we entered was seemingly, in its normal

state, filled with incarnate darkness; even the hot sunlight streaming in through the door seemed to be lost in the vast thickness of the walls, and only showed the masonry rough as when the builder's scaffolding had come down, but coated with dust and marked here and there with patches of dark stain which, if walls could speak, could have given their own dread memories of fear and pain. We were glad to pass up the dusty wooden staircase, the custodian leaving the outer door open to light us somewhat on our way; for to our eyes the one long-wick'd, evil-smelling candle stuck in a sconce on the wall gave an inadequate light. When we came up through the open trap in the corner of the chamber overhead, Amelia held on to me so tightly that I could actually feel her heart beat. I must say for my own part that I was not surprised at her fear, for this room was even more gruesome than that below. Here there was certainly more light, but only just sufficient to realize the horrible surroundings of the place. The builders of the tower had evidently intended that only they who should gain the top should have any of the joys of light and prospect. There, as we had noticed from below, were ranges of windows, albeit of mediaeval smallness, but elsewhere in the tower were only a very few narrow slits such as were habitual in places of mediaeval defense. A few of these only lit the chamber, and these so high up in the wall that from no part could the sky be seen through the thickness of the walls. In racks, and leaning in disorder against the walls, were a number of headsmen's swords, great double-handed weapons with broad blade and keen edge. Hard by were several blocks whereon the necks of the victims had lain, with here and there deep notches where the steel had bitten through the guard of flesh and shored into the wood. Round the chamber, placed in all sorts of irregular ways, were many implements of torture which

made one's heart ache to see—chairs full of spikes which gave instant and excruciating pain; chairs and couches with dull knobs
whose torture was seemingly less, but which, though slower, were
equally efficacious; racks, belts, boots, gloves, collars, all made for
compressing at will; steel baskets in which the head could be slowly
crushed into a pulp if necessary; watchmen's hooks with long handle and knife that cut at resistance—this a specialty of the old Nurnberg police system; and many, many other devices for man's injury
to man. Amelia grew quite pale with the horror of the things, but
fortunately did not faint, for being a little overcome she sat down
on a torture chair, but jumped up again with a shriek, all tendency
to faint gone. We both pretended that it was the injury done to her
dress by the dust of the chair, and the rusty spikes which had upset
her, and Mr. Hutcheson acquiesced in accepting the explanation
with a kind-hearted laugh.

But the central object in the whole of this chamber of horrors
was the engine known as the Iron Virgin, which stood near the
center of the room. It was a rudely-shaped figure of a woman, something of the bell order, or, to make a closer comparison, of the figure
of Mrs. Noah in the children's Ark, but without that slimness of
waist and perfect rondeur of hip which marks the aesthetic type of
the Noah family. One would hardly have recognized it as intended
for a human figure at all had not the founder shaped on the forehead
a rude semblance of a woman's face. This machine was coated with
rust without, and covered with dust; a rope was fastened to a ring
in the front of the figure, about where the waist should have been,
and was drawn through a pulley, fastened on the wooden pillar
which sustained the flooring above. The custodian pulling this rope
showed that a section of the front was hinged like a door at one side;

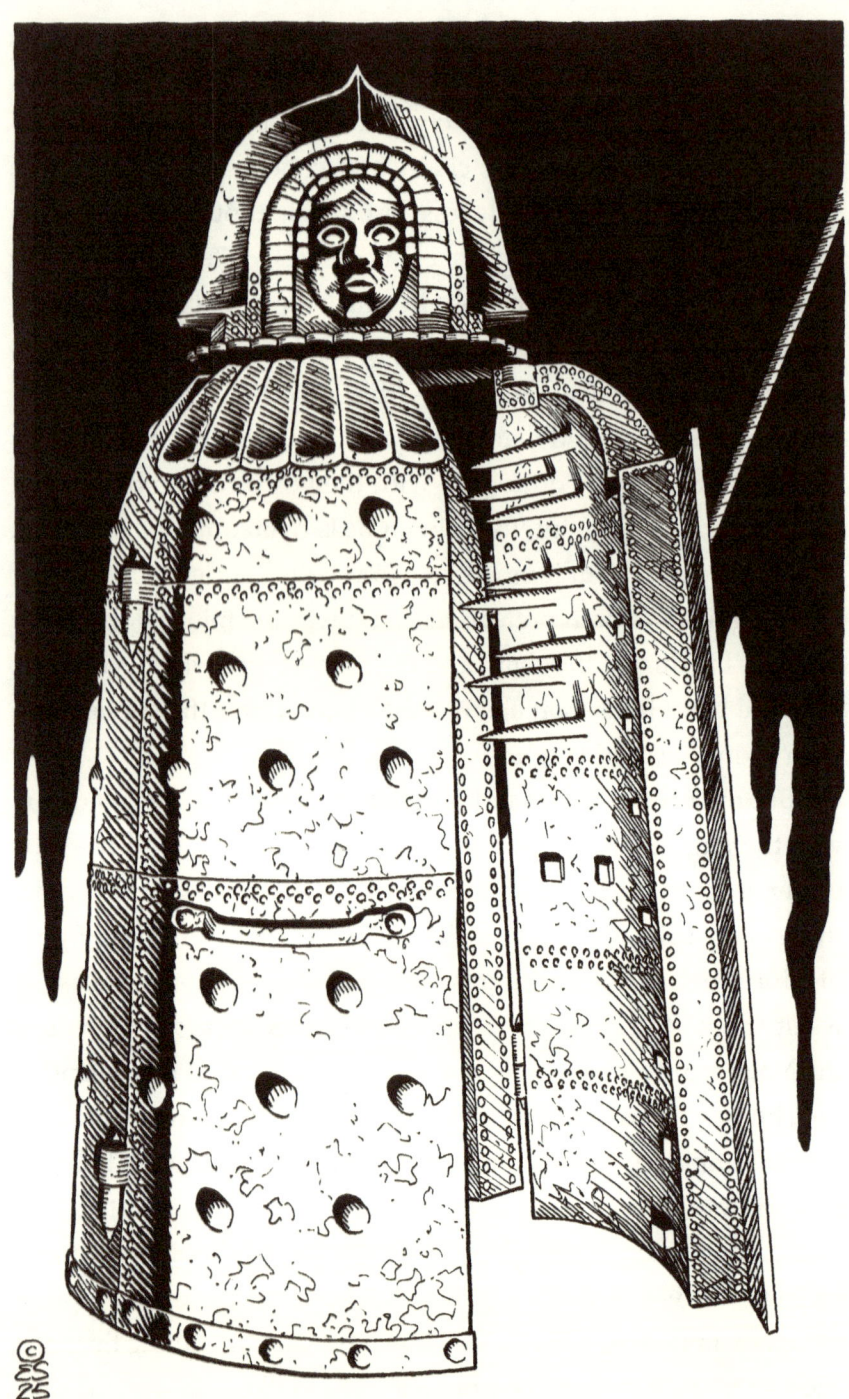

we then saw that the engine was of considerable thickness, leaving just room enough inside for a man to be placed. The door was of equal thickness and of great weight, for it took the custodian all his strength, aided though he was by the contrivance of the pulley, to open it. This weight was partly due to the fact that the door was of manifest purpose hung so as to throw its weight downwards, so that it might shut of its own accord when the strain was released. The inside was honeycombed with rust—nay more, the rust alone that comes through time would hardly have eaten so deep into the iron walls; the rust of the cruel stains was deep indeed! It was only, however, when we came to look at the inside of the door that the diabolical intention was manifest to the full. Here were several long spikes, square and massive, broad at the base and sharp at the points, placed in such a position that when the door should close the upper ones would pierce the eyes of the victim, and the lower ones his heart and vitals. The sight was too much for poor Amelia, and this time she fainted dead off, and I had to carry her down the stairs, and place her on a bench outside till she recovered. That she felt it to the quick was afterwards shown by the fact that my eldest son bears to this day a rude birthmark on his breast, which has, by family consent, been accepted as representing the Nurnberg Virgin.

When we got back to the chamber we found Hutcheson still opposite the Iron Virgin; he had been evidently philosophizing, and now gave us the benefit of his thought in the shape of a sort of exordium.

"Wall, I guess I've been learnin' somethin' here while madam has been gettin' over her faint. 'Pears to me that we're a long way behind the times on our side of the big drink. We uster think out on the plains that the Injun could give us points in tryin' to make a man uncomfortable; but I guess your old mediaeval law-and-order party could raise him every time. Splinters was pretty good in his bluff on the squaw, but this here young miss held a straight flush all high on him. The points of them spikes air sharp enough still, though even the edges air eaten out by what uster be on them. It'd be a good thing for our Indian section to get some specimens of this here play-toy to send round to the Reservations jest to knock the stuffin' out of the bucks, and the squaws too, by showing them as how old civilization lays over them at their best. Guess but I'll get in that box a minute jest to see how it feels!"

"Oh no! no!" said Amelia. "It is too terrible!"

"Guess, ma'am, nothin's too terrible to the explorin' mind. I've been in some queer places in my time. Spent a night inside a dead horse while a prairie fire swept over me in Montana Territory — an' another time slept inside a dead buffler when the Comanches was on the war path an' I didn't keer to leave my kyard on them. I've been two days in a caved-in tunnel in the Billy Broncho gold mine in New Mexico, an' was one of the four shut up for three parts of a day in the caisson what slid over on her side when we was settin' the foundations of the Buffalo Bridge. I've not funked an odd experience yet, an' I don't propose to begin now!"

We saw that he was set on the experiment, so I said: "Well, hurry up, old man, and get through it quick!"

"All right, General," said he, "but I calculate we ain't quite ready yet. The gentlemen, my predecessors, what stood in that thar canister, didn't volunteer for the office — not much! And I guess there was some ornamental tyin' up before the big stroke was made. I want to go into this thing fair and square, so I must get fixed up proper first. I dare say this old galoot can rise some string and tie me up accordin' to sample?"

This was said interrogatively to the old custodian, but the latter, who understood the drift of his speech, though perhaps not appreciating to the full the niceties of dialect and imagery, shook his head. His protest was, however, only formal and made to be overcome. The American thrust a gold piece into his hand, saying: "Take it, pard! it's your pot; and don't be skeer'd. This ain't no necktie party that you're asked to assist in!" He produced some thin frayed rope and proceeded to bind our companion with sufficient strictness for the purpose. When the upper part of his body was bound, Hutcheson said:

"Hold on a moment, Judge. Guess I'm too heavy for you to tote into the canister. You jest let me walk in, and then you can wash up regardin' my legs!"

Whilst speaking he had backed himself into the opening which was just enough to hold him. It was a close fit and no mistake. Amelia looked on with fear in her eyes, but she evidently did not like to say anything. Then the custodian completed his task by tying the American's feet together so that he was now absolutely helpless and fixed in his voluntary prison. He seemed to really enjoy it, and the incipient smile which was habitual to his face blossomed into actuality as he said:

"Guess this here Eve was made out of the rib of a dwarf! There ain't much room for a full-grown citizen of the United States to hustle. We uster make our coffins more roomier in Idaho territory. Now, Judge, you jest begin to let this door down, slow, on to me. I want to feel the same pleasure as the other jays had when those spikes began to move toward their eyes!"

"Oh no! no! no!" broke in Amelia hysterically. "It is too terrible! I can't bear to see it!—I can't! I can't!" But the American was obdurate. "Say, Colonel," said he, "why not take Madame for a little promenade? I wouldn't hurt her feelin's for the world; but now that I am here, havin' kem eight thousand miles, wouldn't it be too hard to give up the very experience I've been pinin' an' pantin' fur? A man can't get to feel like canned goods every time! Me and the Judge here'll fix up this thing in no time, an' then you'll come back, an' we'll all laugh together!"

Once more the resolution that is born of curiosity triumphed, and Amelia stayed holding tight to my arm and shivering whilst the custodian began to slacken slowly inch by inch the rope that held back the iron door. Hutcheson's face was positively radiant as his eyes followed the first movement of the spikes.

"Wall!" he said, "I guess I've not had enjoyment like this since I left Noo York. Bar a scrap with a French sailor at Wapping—an' that warn't much of a picnic neither—I've not had a show fur real pleasure in this dod-rotted Continent, where there ain't no b'ars nor no Injuns, an' wheer nary man goes heeled. Slow there, Judge! Don't you rush this business! I want a show for my money this game—I du!"

The custodian must have had in him some of the blood of his predecessors in that ghastly tower, for he worked the engine with a deliberate and excruciating slowness which after five minutes, in which the outer edge of the door had not moved half as many inches, began to overcome Amelia. I saw her lips whiten, and felt her hold upon my arm relax. I looked around an instant for a place whereon to lay her, and when I looked at her again found that her eye had become fixed on the side of the Virgin. Following its direction, I saw the black cat crouching out of sight. Her green eyes shone like danger lamps in the gloom of the place, and their color was heightened by the blood which still smeared her coat and reddened her mouth. I cried out:

"The cat! look out for the cat!" for even then she sprang out before the engine. At this moment she looked like a triumphant demon. Her eyes blazed with ferocity, her hair bristled out till she seemed twice her normal size, and her tail lashed about as does a tiger's when the quarry is before it. Elias P. Hutcheson when he saw her was amused, and his eyes positively sparkled with fun as he said:

"Darned if the squaw hain't got on all her war paint! Jest give her a shove off if she comes any of her tricks on me, for I'm so fixed everlastingly by the boss, that durn my skin if I can keep my eyes from her if she wants them! Easy there, Judge! don't you slack that 'ar rope or I'm euchered!"

At this moment Amelia completed her faint, and I had to clutch hold of her round the waist or she would have fallen to the floor. Whilst attending to her I saw the black cat crouching for a spring, and jumped up to turn the creature out.

But at that instant, with a sort of hellish scream, she hurled herself, not as we expected at Hutcheson, but straight at the face of the custodian. Her claws seemed to be tearing wildly as one sees in the Chinese drawings of the dragon rampant, and as I looked, I saw one of them light on the poor man's eye, and actually tear through it and down his cheek, leaving a wide band of red where the blood seemed to spurt from every vein.

With a yell of sheer terror which came quicker than even his sense of pain, the man leaped back, dropping as he did so the rope which held back the iron door. I jumped for it, but was too late, for the cord ran like lightning through the pulley-block, and the heavy mass fell forward from its own weight.

As the door closed, I caught a glimpse of our poor companion's face. He seemed frozen with terror. His eyes stared with

a horrible anguish as if dazed, and no sound came from his lips.

And then the spikes did their work. Happily, the end was quick, for when I wrenched open the door, they had pierced so deep that they had locked in the bones of the skull through which they had crushed, and actually tore him—it—out of his iron prison till, bound as he was, he fell at full length with a sickly thud upon the floor, the face turning upward as he fell.

I rushed to my wife, lifted her up and carried her out, for I feared for her very reason if she should wake from her faint to such a scene. I laid her on the bench outside and ran back. Leaning against the wooden column was the custodian moaning in pain whilst he held his reddening handkerchief to his eyes. And sitting on the head of the poor American was the cat, purring loudly as she licked the blood which trickled through the gashed socket of his eyes.

I think no one will call me cruel because I seized one of the old executioner's swords and shore her in two as she sat.

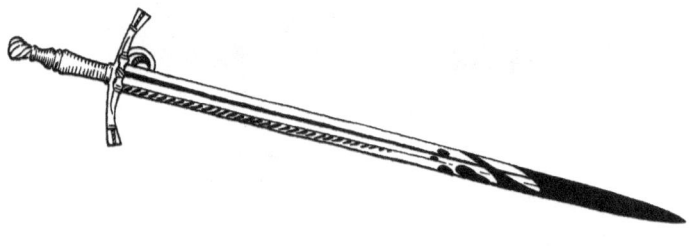

Prolific writer **Abraham "Bram" Stoker** (1847-1912), born in Dublin, Ireland, is remembered today as the author of the classic horror novel *Dracula*. During his lifetime, Stoker was known as the manager of the Lyceum Theatre in London's West End and assistant to that theatre's owner, the celebrated Irish stage actor Henry Irving. Stoker's theatrical career surfaces in his writing. Two examples in this book are "A Star Trap," which immerses the reader in late nineteenth century theatrical life, and "The Squaw," which mentions Irving.

Award-winning cartoonist **Eric Shanower** writes and draws the graphic novel series *Age of Bronze,* a retelling of the Trojan War legend. Shanower's many other comics projects include collaborations with Jean "Moebius" Giraud, Harlan Ellison, and Ed Brubaker. His illustrations grace children's books by L. Frank Baum, Walter R. Brooks, and Eloise Jarvis McGraw.

www.ingramcontent.com/pod-product-compliance
Lightning Source LLC
Chambersburg PA
CBHW030533020726
47494CB00004B/1343